# Struck by Lightning!

The storm seemed to be letting up. Brad slowed down a little. His earlier panic now seemed silly. What was he afraid of, anyway?

He glanced down, thinking how uncomfortable it was to walk in jeans that were soaking wet. The first thing he'd do when he got to his aunt's house—

In that instant, the world exploded around him in a bright, searing flash.

A deafening *boom!* surrounded Brad, sending a knife-like pain shooting deep into his eardrums. He screamed, but in the roar he couldn't hear himself. White light and noise were all around him. Every muscle in his body felt stiff as stone.

*He couldn't move or even breathe!*

Books in the
# Real Kids Real Adventures™
*series*

REAL KIDS, REAL ADVENTURES #1
*A Sudden Shark Attack!*
*A Ski Slope Rescue!*
*A Thirty-Five-Foot Fall!*

REAL KIDS, REAL ADVENTURES #2
*A Rock-Climbing Accident!*
*A Frantic Kidnapper!*
*A Deadly Flood!*

REAL KIDS, REAL ADVENTURES #3
*A Powerful Tornado!*
*A Deadly Riptide!*
*A Wild Bear Attack!*

REAL KIDS, REAL ADVENTURES #4
*A School Bus Out of Control!*
*A Burning Ship!*
*A Deadly Gas!*

REAL KIDS, REAL ADVENTURES #5
*A Lightning Strike!*
*A Shattering Earthquake!*
*A Rope Swing Accident!*

# Real Kids Real Adventures™

NUMBER

## DEBORAH MORRIS

BERKLEY BOOKS, NEW YORK

This is an original publication of The Berkley Publishing Group.

REAL KIDS, REAL ADVENTURES #5:
A LIGHTNING STRIKE!

A Berkley Book / published by arrangement with the author

PRINTING HISTORY
Berkley edition / December 1997

All rights reserved.
Copyright © 1997 by Deborah Morris.
Book design by Casey Hampton
This book may not be reproduced in whole or in part,
by mimeograph or any other means, without permission.
For information address: The Berkley Publishing Group,
a member of Penguin Putnam Inc.,
200 Madison Avenue, New York, New York 10016.

The Putnam Berkley World Wide Web site address is
http://www.berkley.com

ISBN: 0-425-16117-X

**Library of Congress Cataloging-in-Publication Data**

Morris, Deborah, 1956–
    Real kids real adventures / Deborah Morris.—Berkley ed.
    p. cm.
    Originally published: Nashville, Tenn. : Broadman & Holman
Publishers, c1994–<c1995>.
    Contents: 2. Over the edge ; Kidnapped! ; Swept underground—
3. Tornado! ; Hero on the Blanco River ; Bear attack!
    ISBN 0-425-15975-2 (pbk. : v. 2).—ISBN 0-425-16043-2 (pbk. : v. 3)
    1. Christian biography—United States—Juvenile literature.
2. Children—United States—Biography—Juvenile literature.
[1. Survival. 2. Adventure and adventurers. 3. Christian
biography.] I. Title.
[BR1714.M67  1997]                                      97-5391
277.3'082'0922—dc21                                        CIP
    [B]                                                    AC

BERKLEY®
Berkley Books are published by The Berkley Publishing Group,
a member of Penguin Putnam Inc.,
200 Madison Avenue, New York, New York 10016.
BERKLEY and the "B" design
are trademarks belonging to Berkley Publishing Corporation.

PRINTED IN THE UNITED STATES OF AMERICA

10   9   8   7   6   5   4   3   2   1

# A Lightning Strike!

## THE BRAD SMITH STORY

ABOVE: The tree line Brad followed home from fishing.

The unseen creature darted back and forth, leaving a sharp ripple in the water. Brad Smith, sixteen, planted his feet firmly on the pond's grassy bank and yanked. He finally hauled in his prey, a black and silver bass, from the murky water.

"Hey, you're a pretty one," he murmured, hooking his fingers into the flapping fish's gills. The bass wasn't huge, but then again, neither was the pond. Brad pried the hook from its mouth, held it up to admire one more time, then tossed the fish back into the water. It disappeared without a splash.

An avid fisherman, Brad was a sophomore at Muncie Central High School in Muncie, Indiana. He liked fishing the ponds that dotted the fields near his house, but he rarely kept the fish he caught. It was too much work to clean and cook them.

He fished a little while longer, then shoved his gear back into his tackle box. Thunder was rumbling in the distance as he snapped the box shut. He lived about two miles away, past some wooded fields that ran behind the Farm and Fleet store. Farm and Fleet was a square white building perched on a hill above the pond.

Brad propped his fishing rod over his shoulder and started up the hill, trampling the tall grass with each step. He usually cut across Farm and Fleet's gravel parking lot, then angled his way along the trees at the edge of the fields.

Humming under his breath, Brad thought ahead to the weekend. He and some friends were going to the Anderson Speedway on Saturday. They liked to cheer for their favorite race car, number 15, a purple and white Camaro. Sometimes the racetrack owners gave them $10 if they stayed after to help clean up the track.

It started to sprinkle just as Brad reached his house. He stomped his feet as he climbed the porch steps, trying to shake the damp grass clumps off his old Nikes. His mom hated it when he tracked mud on the carpet. If he'd had a brother, he might be able to blame it on him sometimes, but all he had was a twelve-year-old sister. Tracy might be a tomboy, but she didn't usually get dirty.

The bottom of his Nikes were hopelessly caked with mud. Sighing, Brad propped his fishing rod against the wall before squatting to untie his shoes. He was careful with the fishing rod. It was a Berkley Lightning Rod, one of the best money could buy. His dad had given it to him several years before.

The rain became a steady patter. Brad was glad he wasn't still out in it. It ran off the porch roof in sheets, splashing the ground a few feet away. He tugged one shoe off, then reached over to pry the front door open a crack.

"Hey, Dad, are you home?" he yelled.

Tracy's voice drifted back. "He's not here yet, Brad!" The TV was on, and Brad could hear girlish laughter coming from the living room. Tracy must have friends over.

Sure enough, Tracy was watching cartoons with Christy and Casey, two of her best friends. Christy was blond, and Casey was a redhead. They both looked up with big smiles when he walked in.

"Hi, Brad!" they chorused.

Brad shook his head. The place was practically crawling with little girls! "Hey," he grunted in reply. A quick look around told him that the TV remote was missing—as usual—so he walked over to the set. Without asking, he flipped the channel to a basketball game.

That brought Tracy bouncing up from the couch. "Brad!" she said sharply, her brown eyes snapping. "What's your problem? Put it back where it was!"

Brad gave her an amused look. "Aren't you a little old to be watching cartoons? I want to watch the game."

"I don't care. You can't just come in here and change the channel like that!"

Brad looked down at her from his full 5'7" height. "I can't?" he said, matching her gaze with almost identical brown eyes. "Seems to me I just did."

Tracy, furious, looked to Christy and Casey for support, but they both kept silent. Tracy rolled her eyes. They both thought Brad was cute. She didn't know what was wrong with them.

"Let's go to my room," she finally said, turning to storm down the hall. "Brad can watch his dumb basketball game until Mom and Dad come home. Then I'm going to *tell on him!*" She raised her voice to make sure the last few words reached her brother's ears.

In the living room, Brad felt a twinge of guilt. It had been mean of him to change the channel like that. He considered calling Tracy back and telling her she could watch her stupid cartoons, but decided he didn't feel *that* guilty. After all, she did the same thing all the time when their parents were home. He'd be nice to her another day, when he felt like it. *If* he felt like it.

That issue settled, Brad leaned back in his dad's recliner to enjoy the game. Outside, the rain pattered in gusts against the windows. He had made it home just in time.

He was still watching TV when his dad walked in. Ronnie Smith was a crane operator, wiry but strong, with a brown mustache and a shiny bald spot on top of his head. When he wasn't using a crane to lift huge steel beams, he was usually fishing, hunting, or preaching. At one time he had been pastor of a small country church. Now he just filled in for their pastor when he couldn't make it on Sundays.

"Hi, son," Mr. Smith said tiredly, wiping a few raindrops off his bald spot. "How was school today?"

Brad shrugged, his eyes still on the TV. "The usual."

Tracy must have heard their father's voice. "Daddy!" she exclaimed, erupting from the hallway. She ran over and flung her arms around him. "You're home!"

Brad glanced at her through narrowed eyes. She was wearing her "pitiful" look. He had a feeling she was up to no good.

"Christy and Casey and I were watching TV," Tracy said mournfully, "and Brad came in and switched the channel. He didn't even ask." She darted an I-told-you-so look in Brad's direction. "And when I asked him to, he wouldn't put it back."

Mr. Smith glanced over at Brad. "Did you do that?"

Brad shrugged. "Yeah, I guess. But she does it to me all the time. I'll be watching football or the races, and she'll switch it to the Barbie channel or something. You never make *her* turn it back!"

Mr. Smith rubbed his forehead like he was getting a headache. "You two are brother and sister. You know better than to act this way. You're supposed to do unto others as you'd have them do unto you."

Tracy was losing her smug look. "Da-ad!" she whined. "It isn't fair! Aren't you going to make him turn it back?"

Mr. Smith's headache was getting worse. "Brad, just turn it back," he said shortly. "And Tracy, you'd better remember this the next time your brother's watching something special. Now you two hug each other and say you're sorry."

"Da-ad!" they both chorused.

Mr. Smith crossed his arms. "Don't you talk back to me. Both of you march right over here and get it over with. *Now!*"

Brad groaned under his breath, wishing he'd left the stupid TV alone. Tracy rolled her eyes, probably wishing she had stayed back in her room with her friends. They both hated it when their dad did this to them.

Brad spoke first, through clenched teeth: "I'm *sorry,* Tracy."

Tracy glared at him. "Me, too, *Brad.*"

Mr. Smith waited. When neither of them moved, he said, "Now hug each other."

Tracy looked like she'd rather bite Brad than hug him. Brad looked like he was sucking on a lemon. They edged stiffly toward each other, then performed the world's quickest hug.

Mr. Smith nodded. "Now that wasn't so bad, was it?"

Brad was afraid to answer truthfully for fear that

his dad would make them do it over again. Instead he mumbled, "Well, I have other things to do. Gotta go."

His father stopped him before he could escape. "Hold on, there. You *did* pick up those limbs in the yard today like I said to, didn't you? They make our yard look bad."

Brad flinched. He'd done his other chores, but he'd forgotten about the limbs. "Uh . . ." he began.

Luckily, his mom provided a distraction just then by staggering in with her arms full of groceries. Her brown bangs, damp from the rain, had fallen forward into her eyes. She brushed them aside impatiently.

"Brad? There are more bags in the car. Can I get you to carry them inside for me?"

"Sure!" he said. He shot out the door, glad to avoid his father's questions. There was always tomorrow, he told himself. He'd get up early and pick up the limbs then.

Mrs. Smith was putting away frozen food when Brad brought in the last few bags. "Thanks, honey. How was school today?"

His mom and dad *always* asked that. He wondered if they even listened to his answers. He was sometimes tempted to say: "Oh, an alien spaceship landed, kidnapped the principal, and blew up the school building, but other than that, not much." Chances were they'd both say "That's nice."

"It was okay," he replied. "I passed my math test.

Oh, and Derrick and Wendell and I made plans to go to the Anderson Speedway tomorrow."

"That's nice," Mrs. Smith said absently, putting ice cream in the freezer. "Here, can you pass me the frozen peas? They should be in that bag right in front of you."

Brad rooted around until he found the cold, knobbly bag of peas, then grasped it like a football. When his mom looked up, he grinned.

"Ready?" he asked, pulling his hand back over his shoulder. He was going to "pass" the peas!

She laughed. "Okay, silly, hand them over!"

Brad took careful aim, then sent the peas sailing across the kitchen. Mrs. Smith snatched at them and missed. They hit the floor like a—well, like a sack of frozen peas.

"Oops," she said, stooping to pick them up. "At least the bag didn't break."

Brad grabbed more frozen food and carried it over to her. "Don't ever try out for football," he advised her kindly, as he helped her. "You'd never make it."

"Oh, rats. And here I thought pro football might be my next career." Mrs. Smith closed the freezer door, then turned quickly to cup Brad's face in her ice-cold hands.

"Hey!" he yelped, backing away from her. "Quit that! You're freezing me."

"Good. That's what you get for throwing my peas on the floor."

The storm outside was getting worse. Brad was glad now that he had forgotten to pick up the limbs. The way the wind was blowing, more branches would be down by morning. He would've had to do it all over again.

Brad gripped the gray metal fence, screaming his lungs out. A thunderous roar drowned out his voice.

"Go, number 15! Get past them!"

Driver Rick Ronomous's purple Camaro roared past on the racetrack below, blocked behind three other "late models." As they turned the corner on the oval track, a cloud of smelly exhaust fumes floated into the crowd. Brad shook the fence in frustration. If car 15 was going to win, it needed to break out of the pack and get to the front!

It was Saturday evening at the Anderson Speedway, and Brad's throat was already sore from screaming. That morning, picking up soggy limbs outside his house, he had been afraid the races would get cancelled because of rain. Despite cloudy skies all day, though, no storm had moved in.

Wendell and Derrick had gone to the refreshment stand to buy Cokes. When they returned, Brad followed them back up to his seat. Sometimes he liked standing at the fence where he could look straight down at the track, but it was easier to see the whole racecourse from the bleachers.

"What'd we miss?" Wendell asked, handing Brad a drink. "Any good wrecks?"

Brad didn't take his eyes off the track. "No. Rick is still locked in third place." Car 51 was a blue and orange Camaro that often won. Car 88 was a burgundy Monte Carlo. Both of them were ahead of number 15 at the moment.

Rick Ronomous finally managed to pass 88, but when the checkered flag came out, it was number 51 that crossed the line first. Rick took a respectable second place. It was a good race, even if their favorite didn't win.

They watched several more races, then decided to call it a night. None of them needed $10 enough this week to clean up after all the slobs who threw their paper cups and other trash on the ground. Besides, the ground was still mushy from all the rain.

On the way home, Brad's thoughts drifted lazily to the week ahead. Another long week of school, he thought with a sigh. There were thousands of things he'd rather do than sit in a classroom all day. If he wasn't in school, he could—

He stopped his thoughts right there. Not a good idea to start thinking like that, he warned himself. Remember the huge trouble you got into last time?

It had happened the previous October, soon after school had started. Brad and his buddy, Brandy, both liked to bow-hunt. One Sunday afternoon, after spending hours stalking through the woods with their bows, they had finally spotted some deer. By then it was getting dark, so they had to quit and go home.

Brad had grumbled all the way back to Brandy's car. "This stinks," he said, tossing his bow into the trunk. "We could come back tomorrow and bag one if we didn't have school."

Thinking back, Brad was practically sure that the next part had been Brandy's idea . . . but maybe it had been his. At any rate, somehow or other the two of them had decided to "forget school" the next day and hunt instead.

Once that decision had been made, they started making plans.

"My mom's always home in the mornings," Brad had said. "I think it'll be a little obvious if I stroll out to the bus wearing my old clothes and carrying my hunting bow."

"Why don't you bring your bow and a change of clothes over to my house tonight?" Brandy suggested. "You can leave your house at the normal time and come here. In the afternoon, you can change clothes and go home. As long as you leave and come back at the right times, nobody will know the difference."

It had seemed like a perfect plan.

The next morning, Brad had risen at his usual time and dressed for school. He felt guilty, but he felt excited, too. He watched the clock nervously. When 7:15 finally came, he jumped up.

"Bye, Mom!" he called. "I'm leaving! For the bus!" He cringed as he heard himself. He already *sounded* guilty, even though he hadn't—technically—done anything wrong yet. He felt like a big flashing sign that said "LIAR!" was hanging over his head.

"Bye, honey. Have a good day!" Apparently, his mom couldn't see the sign. Brad mumbled a reply and slid out the door, unable to meet her eyes.

Once he was outside, though, the guilty feeling evaporated. Freedom! This was going to be great. He ran over to Brandy's house, and after a quick change of clothes, the two headed for their Happy Hunting Ground.

They had fun, even though they never came close enough to a deer to even yell at it, much less shoot it. Before they knew it, it was time to go home. School would be letting out in an hour.

Brad changed back into his school clothes at Brandy's. When the bus pulled up to let students out, he strolled out and joined the crowd. Perfect!

It stayed perfect until he walked in the front door. His dad was inside waiting for him, and he looked like a volcano ready to explode. A small voice in Brad's mind said: *Uh-oh.*

He twisted his face into a smile. "Hi, Dad," he said. He felt like the smile was frozen on his face. The "LIAR!" sign was back. It was hanging right above his head again. His palms were suddenly damp.

Mr. Smith looked at him, then asked in a purring voice, "How was your day at school, son?"

Brad swallowed nervously. "I guess it was all right."

"Oh, was it? That's interesting. That's *really* interesting since you didn't even *go* to school today!" Mr. Smith's voice was now a roar, and the big vein on the side of his neck was throbbing.

Brad froze, staring at his dad like a deer caught in the headlights. "I—I—, uh—"

"You *what*? Skipped school? Lied to your mother and me?"

That hadn't been exactly what Brad had planned to say. His mind raced, trying to come up with an excuse that would work. Amnesia? Sickness? An emergency?

His father wasn't waiting for an excuse. "You know better than this!" he shouted. "When I was young, both my parents died. I didn't *get* to finish school. Yet here you are, with an opportunity I never had, and what do you do?" He paused for breath, then demanded, "Answer me!"

Brad felt sick to his stomach. "Uh—"

"You skip school, that's what you do! I can't believe it. *My* son, skipping school!"

Brad's mouth was dry. "I—I'm sorry, Dad."

"Sorry?" Mr. Smith sounded incredulous. "*Sorry?* How do you think it made your mother feel when your school beeped her at work to ask where you were?"

So that's how they found out, Brad thought numbly. Any hope of appealing to his mom for mercy disappeared. She'd be twice as mad as his dad.

Brad licked his dry lips. "It won't happen again."

Mr. Smith just glared at him. "You better believe it won't happen again. And just to make sure of it, I'm going to keep you busy for a while. Starting tomorrow, you're going to bring home every one of your schoolbooks every day. Then you're going to spend your afternoons studying at the kitchen table. No fishing, no friends, nothing but books. You can forget our hunting trip next weekend, too."

Brad's mouth fell open. "But Dad—"

His father's expression stopped him. "Don't even try it. I want you to remember this, because if you ever pull something like this again . . ." He let the threatening sentence trail off.

Now, almost seven months later, Brad still cringed when he remembered his father's face that day. He'd never been brave enough—or stupid enough—to find out what would happen if he tried to skip school again. It had taken a long time to earn back his dad's respect, and he didn't plan to lose it again.

The next morning was a Sunday. Brad dragged himself out of bed at nine o'clock, still groggy from the late night at the Speedway. He groped around in his closet for pants and a shirt, then started getting dressed. He buttoned his shirt with his eyes half-closed and ended up with a leftover button. He wished Sunday School started at a decent hour, like maybe late afternoon. Maybe by then he could button a shirt straight.

He didn't really wake up until he was sitting in class an hour later. His Sunday School teacher was talking about the Ten Commandments, which Brad was pretty sure he had covered. You weren't supposed to steal, murder people, lie, commit adultery . . .

He frowned. How many was that? Four? Maybe he didn't know them as well as he thought. How'd he lose six whole commandments? He sat up straighter and tried to pay attention.

Later, eating lunch with his family, he was glad he had listened. When his dad asked about the lesson that morning, Brad was able to rattle off all *ten* commandments without hesitation. His dad was impressed.

"Good for you," Mr. Smith said. "It always takes me a minute to remember all ten. You got your old man beat."

Brad grinned. He thought about confessing that he'd forgotten six of the commandments at first, but why ruin his image?

"Yeah," he said modestly. "Well, you kinda drilled them into me when I was a kid. Every time we were working or fishing, you'd always be talking about that stuff."

His father looked skeptical. "I never remember talking to you about the Ten Commandments while we were fishing. What would I say, 'Hey, that's a nice bass . . . kind of reminds me of the fifth commandment: Honor your father and mother'?"

Brad laughed. "No, it was probably more like the one that says, 'You shall not covet' the huge bass your son caught!"

Mrs. Smith stifled a smile. "I think he got you, Ronnie."

"I think you're right." Mr. Smith chuckled and shook his head. "Maybe I'd better stop taking him fishing. Or to church."

"Uh-huh," said Brad. "I'll pass out the day you tell me *not* to go to church!"

His father ignored the comment. "Speaking of fishing," he said brightly, "I was talking to Louie this morning about going out to Summit Lake after work on Tuesday. You want to come?"

Louie was an old preacher friend of Mr. Smith's. He often took Brad and Mr. Smith out in his fishing boat. Summit Lake was about twenty minutes away.

Brad shook his head. "Thanks, but I don't think so. I'm gonna stick around here and maybe fish one of the ponds."

"Well then, boy, why don't you come with us? It'll be better fishing out on the lake."

"Probably so, but I'm in the mood to be by myself. Thanks anyway." Brad stood up and dug his truck keys out of his pocket. "I promised Jason I'd go over to his house this afternoon to play some basketball. He's probably waiting for me."

Tracy jumped up hopefully. "Can I go along and play with you guys?"

Brad rolled his eyes. "No. And don't go following me over there, either. We play rough, and you'd just end up with a black eye or something."

Tracy's face fell, and once again Brad felt a twinge of guilt. Tracy really wasn't all that bad. Sometimes when he was in a hurry to go somewhere, she finished his chores for him so he could leave. He resolved to be nicer to her—but not today. There would be plenty of time later.

Tuesday morning dawned clear and bright. Brad got ready for school and went out to wait for the bus. The sun felt good on his face and shoulders.

The school day seemed to last forever. Between each class, Brad stared outside longingly. It was hard to concentrate on his work when the sun was shining and a cool spring breeze was tickling the trees. It was a perfect day for fishing.

When school finally let out, Brad grabbed his friend Eric in the hall. "Hey, can I catch a ride home with you today? I want to get home early so I can go fishing."

Eric shrugged. "Sure. Come on."

Ten minutes later, Brad was standing in his front yard, waving at the back of Eric's car. Now all he had to do was zip through his afternoon chores, change clothes, and go. Maybe he could bribe Tracy into helping out. Sometimes she'd wash dishes or vacuum for him if he gave her a dollar.

Since Tracy wouldn't get home from school for another half hour, though, Brad decided he'd better get started. He changed into grass-stained jeans and an old Duke University T-shirt, then grabbed a dust rag. He slapped it half heartedly at the furniture and lamp shades, sending dust specks swirling into the air. What was the point? It would all just land somewhere else.

The minute he heard the front door slam, he called out, "Tracy? That you?"

"Yeah," his sister replied. He heard a thump as she dropped her school books on the kitchen table, then she walked into the living room. "What do you want?"

"You want to earn a dollar? I already dusted, but if you'll vacuum for me, I'll pay you."

Tracy considered it. "Only if you pay me *first*. You always promise to pay me, then after I finish the work, you don't."

Brad dug in his jeans pocket and fished out a crumpled dollar bill. He slapped it onto her palm. "Fine. Here's your dollar. Just make sure you do it before Mom gets home."

"Okay."

Another door slammed and Ronnie Smith walked in. "Hi, kids," he said. "You two fighting today?"

"No, Daddy," Tracy said sweetly, shoving Brad's dollar bill into her pocket. "We were just talking."

"That's good. Just wanted to make sure you didn't

need to hug each other again," he added, with a twinkle in his eye.

"Everything's great," Brad said hastily. "I was about to go fishing down at the pond."

"Why don't you come along with Louie and me? We're heading out to Summit Lake here in a few minutes. Come on, son. It'll be a lot better fishing out in Louie's boat."

Brad wasn't in the mood. "I'm just gonna stick around here."

Mr. Smith shrugged. "Okay, but you'll be missing out. If you change your mind, you can try catching us at Louie's."

Brad nodded, then glanced at the clock. It was already after four. After his dad left, he gathered his fishing gear and called Sheldon, a friend in the neighborhood, to ask for a lift. He hated to waste the time it would take to walk to the pond.

A few minutes later, Sheldon pulled up in his old Chevelle and honked the horn. Brad was waiting. "Hey!" he greeted Sheldon, sliding his tackle box and fishing rod into the back. "Thanks for picking me up."

"No problem. I was going out anyway. Where do you want to get dropped?"

"Over by Farm and Fleet. I caught some bass there the other night."

In a car, the whole trip took less than two minutes. When the Chevelle bumped to a stop in the gravel parking lot, Brad quickly unfolded himself from the passenger seat.

"Hey, thanks again," he said, easing out his tackle box and rod. "You saved me a long walk."

His friend grinned. "Hope you catch something other than chiggers." He took off with a wave and a spurt of gravel.

Propping the Berkley Lightning Rod over one shoulder, Brad hefted his tackle box and started down toward the pond. The sun felt warm on his shoulders, and the gravel scrunched under his Nikes with each step. He felt good.

He hiked and slithered down the small hill. The pond was bright blue, reflecting the sky. Thick trees grew down to the water in several places. Brad picked a comfortable spot on the bank, opened his tackle box, and picked out a Rattlin' Rogue lure.

Rattlin' Rogues looked like small, mutant fish dangling with hooks. They were hollow, with small beads inside that rattled as they were pulled through the water. The noise often made fish curious enough to bite. Brad hoped a lot of curious bass were cruising around underwater.

He tied on the lure and cast it out smoothly. It landed with a wet plunk and sank out of sight. Brad waited a moment, then started reeling it in slowly.

On his fourth or fifth cast, he got his first bite. He pulled in a small bass, unhooked it, and tossed it back. He kept fishing, slowly working his way around the pond. In less than an hour, he landed three largemouth bass.

A sudden breeze riffled the water, catching Brad's attention. He looked up, noticing for the first time that the sun had slipped behind some clouds. He peered around quickly, wondering if a storm was moving in. If so, he'd need to head home.

But none of the clouds were black, and there was no rumble of thunder. He shrugged. It must just be getting dark earlier than usual.

The bass were *really* starting to bite. Brad reeled in fish after fish as he worked his way along the grassy bank. He was concentrating so much on fishing that he didn't notice the line of storm clouds scudding toward him across the darkening sky.

Fifteen miles away, out in the middle of Summit Lake, Ronnie Smith and Louie were also getting a lot of bites. The boat was drifting along with the current, the engine off. Mr. Smith reeled his line in slowly, ready to give it a jerk if he got a nibble.

It wasn't until a surprisingly cold breeze swept across the lake that he looked up at the sky. What he saw made him give a long whistle.

"Hey, Louie, take a look at that," he said, pointing. A long line of dark clouds had formed in the distance. As they both watched, a flash of lightning danced sideways across the sky, hopping from cloud to cloud. A few seconds later, they heard the faint rumble of thunder.

Louie wrinkled his forehead in thought. "Maybe

it'll blow over before it gets here. Let's wait and see what happens. If it keeps coming this way, we can head in."

"That's probably why the fish are biting so good," Mr. Smith said. "Just before a storm, they always hit. It's like they turn on." He cast out his line and was soon reeling in another bass.

They kept fishing, keeping a close eye on the sky. The wind picked up and the lake grew choppy. The flickers of lightning and the answering thunder were getting closer.

Finally Louie sighed. "I think it's time to get off the lake, Ronnie. I don't want to get lightning-struck out here."

Mr. Smith squinted at the sky, then nodded. "Well, it's sure messed up some good fishing," he grumbled as he put away his fishing tackle. "Let's head on back to the house."

"Yes!" exclaimed Brad as he felt a sharp tug on his line. He had another fish hooked, and it felt big. This would be his fifth catch of the afternoon.

He wrestled his fishing rod, his eyes on the water. He had the fish halfway to shore when he realized how dark and choppy the water had become. What had happened to the sunny, blue sky?

But he didn't have time to worry about that right now—not with a lively fish causing his rod to bend almost in half. It took him another minute or so to land it. It was another largemouth bass. He threw it back, then looked up at the sky.

He was surprised to see how gray it had become. The sun was still visible overhead, but off in the distance, he could see a line of dark clouds moving toward him. When a low growl of thunder sounded, Brad realized he'd been hearing it for a while. It just hadn't registered in his brain as important. He had been too intent on fishing.

Now, seeing lightning flicker through the clouds in the distance, he decided it was time to go. He had always been a little scared of thunder . . . not to mention that he had to walk all the way home. He didn't want to get caught in a storm.

He stuffed everything back into his tackle box and stood up. A gust of cold air raised goosebumps on his arms, bringing with it the smell of rain.

"Oh, great," Brad muttered to himself. "I'm gonna get soaked." Propping his fishing rod over his left shoulder, he grabbed the tackle box and started up the hill toward the Farm and Fleet store.

A loud boom of thunder startled him just as he reached the top. He walked faster, looking back over his shoulder at the line of storm clouds. They were a *lot* closer than they had been just minutes before. He would never make it home before the storm broke.

He thought quickly. His aunt's house was closer, just a six- or seven-minute walk. Brad decided to go there instead. He broke into a shuffling run, the tackle box banging painfully against his right leg.

He had just started across the open field behind Farm and Fleet when a raindrop splatted in his face. He tried to hurry even faster, but within seconds the drizzle turned into a downpour. Soon his T-shirt and jeans were soaked.

He could hardly see where he was going. Blinking rapidly, he peered ahead through the gray rain. Suddenly the whole field was lit up by a blinding flash of lightning, followed by a thunderous roar. Brad gasped. That was *close*!

He stumbled across the uneven ground, trying to ignore the pounding of his heart. He really hated thunderstorms. They always left him feeling like some scared little kid.

*I need to get to the trees on the other side,* he thought. *I can work my way along the edge of the field and stay out of the rain.*

Lightning streaked down again, seeming to strike almost beside Brad. The thunder that followed shook the ground under his feet and left his chest vibrating. Panicked, Brad ran wildly, hoping he was still heading in the right direction. He did *not* want to be in an open field with lightning popping all around him!

He was relieved when he saw the outline of trees towering through the gloom ahead. He was almost there! He put on another burst of speed, setting his lures and hooks rattling. When he reached the trees, he ran under their shelter gratefully. Rain was still drizzling down through the leaves and branches overhead, but it was a lot drier than being out in the open.

Lightning flashed again, followed by an ear-piercing "*cr-aa-ack!*" of thunder. Brad jumped, but he felt safer now that he was out of the field. He gripped his tackle box and fishing rod tighter and started making his way along the treeline toward his aunt's house.

The storm seemed to be letting up. Brad slowed down a little. His earlier panic now seemed silly. What was he afraid of, anyway?

He glanced down, thinking how uncomfortable it was to walk in jeans that were soaking wet. The first thing he'd do when he got to his aunt's house—

In that instant, the world exploded around him in a bright, searing flash.

A deafening *boom!* surrounded Brad, sending a knife-like pain shooting deep into his eardrums. He screamed, but in the roar he couldn't hear himself. White light and noise were all around him. Every muscle in his body felt stiff as stone. He couldn't move or even breathe.

Helpless to resist, Brad felt himself being lifted off the ground. The air around him quivered with pure white heat, and the sharp smell of burning flesh filled his nostrils. If he could have moved, he would have gagged.

Finally, like a toy tossed aside by a giant, Brad felt himself being tossed backward. His body slammed to the ground beneath the trees, knocking out his breath.

After that came blackness.

"Wow! Louie, did you hear that?" Mr. Smith peered across the lake to the north, where the storm was gathering force. Lightning was streaking down almost nonstop, and the thunder was impressive even miles away.

Louie was steering the boat toward shore. "Yeah. We need to get this boat out of the water. The storm's still moving this way."

"I'm with you, buddy," Mr. Smith said sincerely. "That's getting a little too close for comfort."

Brad moaned. He was lying on his back, his legs bent and sprawled out like a frog's legs. When he opened his eyes, he saw what looked like a huge, black spiderweb in the tree branches above him. Rain was dripping down on him, but he couldn't feel anything. His whole body was numb.

At first he couldn't remember what had happened . . . then, piece by piece, the whole thing came back to him.

"No way," he mumbled in disbelief. "I just got hit by lightning!" His chest felt heavy, making it hard to breathe. There was something wrong with his ears, too. They were ringing, and it felt like they were stopped up.

His heart began to thud in fear. Now that he was fully conscious, a flood of sensations hit him all at once.

His arms and hands were tingling.

His head was tingling. It felt like worms were crawling all over it, or that his hair was moving.

He couldn't feel his legs.

It left him in a panic. "God, please let me be all right!" he cried aloud. His voice sounded strange and far away. It was clear that he *wasn't* all right.

Fighting rising fear, Brad used his tingling hands and arms to push himself up into a sitting position. He stared at his legs, willing them desperately to move. Nothing happened. He grabbed them and pinched them as hard as he could, but it was like they weren't even a part of his body.

"God, please help me!" he sobbed again. Forcing himself to act, he picked up his lifeless legs and straightened them. They felt like logs. He saw with horror that his jeans had rips going down his left leg: long, bursting-open tears like the Incredible Hulk's clothes. What did his leg look like?

His eyes moved down to his left foot. His tennis shoe was also mangled and charred, the whole side blown out. The shoestrings were even melted. Brad shuddered and looked away.

Then he saw an odd-looking object on the ground nearby. It was his Berkley Lightning Rod—or what was left of it. Only the handle and a short stub were left. A tangled web of charred fibers lay on the ground nearby. Brad slowly lifted his eyes to the black "spiderweb" in the branches above him. It was his melted fishing rod! It must have blown up and splattered into the branches when the lightning struck.

*I need help,* Brad thought numbly. *I've got to get out of these trees where somebody will see me.*

Since his legs wouldn't move, he decided he'd have to scoot backward, dragging his useless legs. He used his arms to push himself into position, then started scooting himself across the wet ground. It took a lot of work to cross the ten feet to the edge of the trees. It was still raining steadily. Feeling weak and scared, Brad took a deep breath, then dragged himself out into the rain, heading toward the Farm and Fleet store.

"Sir? Is your name Ronnie Smith?"

Mr. Smith was standing next to the boat ramp, his cap pulled low. He and Louie had just finished tying down the boat. He turned to look in surprise at the young Lake Patrol officer.

"Yeah, that's me," he replied.

"Well, sir, we got a message that you need to call home right away. You can use our phone if you want."

"What's happened? Who called?"

"I'm not sure. But I think you'd better hurry."

Alarmed, Mr. Smith followed the officer. In the distance, thunder rumbled and echoed. For reasons he couldn't explain, the sound left him deeply afraid.

"Help! Help me!"

Brad was so weak that it took all his strength just to shout. He had dragged himself in the direction of the Farm and Fleet store until he could see a guy working outside. He waved his still-tingling arms in the air, trying to attract his attention.

Finally, the man looked up. He seemed to hesitate for a moment, then he began to run through the rain toward Brad. Several other people came outside to stare.

The man puffed up and kneeled on the wet ground next to Brad. "What happened?" he asked, staring at Brad's ripped jeans and melted Nikes.

Brad could hardly hear him. It sounded like he was talking from a distance. "I was h-hit by lightning," he stammered. His hair still felt like it was moving by itself. Everything was dream-like. He wanted to drift off to sleep.

"Okay, you're gonna be all right," the man said, jerking Brad back to attention. "But we're gonna need some help." Turning back toward Farm and Fleet, he yelled to the others, "Call an ambulance! The boy's been struck by lightning!"

The man helped Brad lay down. Soon several of the store workers ran up carrying a sheet of plastic.

Together, they held the plastic over Brad to keep the rain off him.

"Everything's going to be fine," one lady said. "An ambulance is on the way."

Brad nodded, too tired to answer. They all sounded like they were a million miles away.

The ambulance arrived a few minutes later. Brad noticed wearily that the sirens didn't sound very loud either. They were like little Hot Wheels sirens. Something was wrong with his ears.

Before he had time to think about it, though, the ambulance workers were bending over him. "Can you hear me?" a man asked. Brad nodded. He saw somebody else tugging at his toasted Nikes, pulling them off. It was strange to see them touching his legs but not *feel* their touch.

Once his shoes and socks were off, the emergency workers used scissors to cut his jeans down both sides. Brad would normally be embarrassed, but there was too much going on. He watched almost with interest as they whisked his jeans away to reveal his legs.

The first glance turned Brad's stomach to stone. His left foot was a dark, nasty purple color, with a burn across it that looked like a whip mark. Long, open burns snaked up his left leg. It was bruised and swollen, like a giant hot dog that had burned and split open.

Brad paled and closed his eyes. I'm hurt bad, he

thought. I can't believe this is happening. He laid still as the emergency workers lifted him onto a stretcher and slid him into the ambulance.

Inside the ambulance, he realized that someone was leaning over him. "What's your mom and dad's phone number, son?"

·Brad had a hard time thinking at first. "My dad's fishing out at Summit Lake," he finally said. He had to shout to hear himself. "My mom's probably on her way home from work. I can give you the number of her car phone."

The ambulance lurched, and the siren started again. Brad tried not to think about his legs. Instead he thought about his mom and dad, and Tracy. What if he died? He didn't know what he'd do if he couldn't see his family anymore. You were supposed to be happy in heaven, but he knew he'd miss his family no matter what.

His throat grew tight. He was fighting back tears when a burning pain suddenly swept across his stomach like a blowtorch. The fiery sensation spread up his chest and down his arms until he felt like his whole body was on fire. He had to bite his lip to keep from screaming.

*Help me,* he prayed silently. *Help me make it. I don't want to leave my family.*

The rest of the trip to the hospital passed in a blur. Brad was only half-conscious when they arrived at Ball Memorial Hospital. He was vaguely aware of people all around him, running and shouting orders.

". . . airlift him to Methodist."

"Morphine . . ."

". . . going into shock."

Their voices all sounded muffled, like they were talking underwater. Brad kept his eyes closed. The next thing he knew, he was being loaded into a helicopter. He wondered where his mom and dad were. Did they know what had happened yet?

*They'll be so upset if I die,* Brad thought feverishly. *I can't do that to them. I've got to make it.*

The helicopter whisked Brad away to the Intensive Care Unit at Methodist Hospital. The pain in his stomach was getting worse. He barely noticed as the nurses stuck needles and tubes into his arms and legs. He was grateful now that he couldn't feel his legs. If they were hurting as bad as the rest of him, he didn't think he could take it without crying.

He didn't know how long he had been there when he heard his mother gasp, "Oh, Brad!" He dragged his eyes open to see her bending over him, tears streaming down her face.

"Hi, Mom," he croaked. It was hard to talk. His neck and throat were burning.

"Honey, are you okay?" Mrs. Smith reached out to touch his arm, then drew her hand back. Brad was wrapped in bandages almost from head to toe.

"I'll be all right." Brad didn't know if that was true or not, but he didn't like seeing his mom cry.

A few minutes later, his dad came running in. Mr.

Smith was still wearing his fishing clothes. When he saw Brad wrapped up like a mummy and bristling with tubes, the blood drained from his face. He hugged his wife, then walked to Brad's bedside.

"Son? I'm here. I love you." Brad could hardly hear his voice. Mr. Smith leaned down to hug him. It was an "air hug," since they barely touched, but it made Brad feel good.

"I'll be all right, Dad," he said in a whisper.

Mr. Smith nodded, then slowly went down on one knee. Leaning his forehead against the side of Brad's bed, he began to pray.

Brad drifted off to sleep, comforted by the familiar voice and words.

The next morning, a doctor came in to talk to Brad and his parents. It had been a long and painful night for Brad, but he had survived. He was pretty sure now that he wasn't going to die. But what about his legs? He still had no feeling in them.

"Am I going to be able to walk again?" he asked the doctor. "Or are my legs going to stay like this?"

The doctor looked grim. "It's too early to tell. Lightning can do strange things. It can shut down your central nervous system and leave you partially paralyzed, but a few days later everything can suddenly return to normal. We're hoping that that's going to happen with you."

"What about my left leg?" Brad asked. "I saw it

when they cut off my jeans. It looked *bad* . . . like it was cooked or something."

Mr. and Mrs. Smith glanced at each other. Brad caught the exchange, and it scared him. What had the doctor told them?

"Well," the doctor said carefully, "you've got second- and third-degree burns on your left leg. It looks like the lightning bolt entered somewhere around your left shoulder and exited from your left foot. It did some damage to muscles and nerves as it passed through your body."

"My jeans leg looked like the Incredible Hulk's clothes. It was ripped apart at the seams."

"Your skin was wet from the rain when you got hit. When the lightning passed down through your left leg, it probably turned that dampness on your skin to steam. The escaping steam blew apart the demim. That's what it looks like, anyway." He paused, then added, "It also seems to have ruptured your left eardrum."

Brad nodded. So *that* was why everything sounded so far away! "I was carrying my fishing rod on my left shoulder when I got hit," he rasped. "My pole got melted."

The doctor raised an eyebrow. "If the lightning had hit your head instead of your fishing pole, you probably wouldn't be here right now. Your pole must've acted like a lightning rod."

Brad was drifting off to sleep again. "It *was* a

Lightning Rod," he murmured. He was asleep before he could hear the doctor's response.

Waking up hours later, Brad was confused. Where was he? He tried to sit up, but the movement made him gasp with pain. It also brought back the reason why he was in the hospital. His parents weren't in the room, so he didn't have to pretend to be cheerful. He looked down at his bandaged legs.

"Why don't you move?" he hissed at them. Gritting his teeth, he mentally commanded his right toes to wiggle.

To his amazement, his toes obediently twitched.

His mouth fell open. "Hey!" he yelled to the empty room. "I can move my toes!" He tried again, wanting to make sure it wasn't an accident. Once again his toes twitched. He still couldn't feel his legs or feet, but if his toes were starting to work, maybe the rest would follow.

By the time his parents and Tracy showed up, Brad was almost bouncing with excitement. "Watch this!" he said, pointing to his feet. When his toes curled, his mom and Tracy both squealed. Brad felt like he'd just won an Olympic medal.

"I knew you'd be okay," Mr. Smith said, beaming. "You're going to be up out of that bed in no time, goofing off on your chores and arguing with your sister."

Brad grinned at him, then turned to Tracy. "How're you doing, Trace?"

His sister had dark circles under her eyes. "Okay, I guess," she said in a small voice. "I couldn't sleep last night. I was afraid something was going to happen to you."

Brad stared at her in surprise. He'd always thought Tracy would be glad if he suddenly disappeared off the face of the earth. Come to think of it, he'd always thought *he* would be glad if *Tracy* suddenly disappeared . . . but now he knew that that wasn't true. He waved her closer.

"I'm going to be all right," he said. "So you stop worrying, okay?" He paused, then added, "Besides, you'd better enjoy hogging the TV while you can. As soon as I get home, it's all mine."

That made her smile. "I don't think so. We can take turns, though."

"Good enough." Brad's eyes were getting heavy again. He yawned. "I think I'm going to take a nap. I'll talk to you guys later."

He was smiling inside as he watched his family leave. It was funny, he thought sleepily, that a bolt of lightning could make Tracy act so sisterly. The next time he was playing basketball, maybe he'd invite her along . . .

Throughout the next day, Brad experimented with his legs, trying again and again to stand. Sweat beaded on his forehead as he put weight on his sore legs. The first few times, the pain was so bad that he had to quit. By late that afternoon, though, he was able to stand on his own.

It was like a party that night when his family and friends showed up to visit. They all clapped and cheered when Brad wiggled carefully out of bed and stood up.

LEFT: What is left of Brad's Berkley Lightning Rod.
BELOW: Brad's ripped jeans, showing where the lightning bolt left his body.

"Thanks," Brad said, a little embarrassed. "I think they're going to let me go home tomorrow. I can't wait!"

"It'll be good to have you back, son," Mr. Smith said. "The house has been quiet without you."

"Yeah," Tracy said. "I've sort of missed you, too. Can you believe it?"

Brad laughed. "What's wrong with you? You crazy?"

"I don't know. It just isn't the same without you." Tracy cleared her throat. "I love you, Brad."

Brad blinked, and his parents smiled at each other. He opened his mouth, and before he knew it, words popped out.

"I love you too, Trace."

Being struck by lightning *definitely* made some strange things happen.

*Brad Smith fully regained his ability to walk, but suffered a permanent forty percent hearing loss in his left ear. He still likes to fish, and he still doesn't like thunderstorms.*

# A Shattering Earthquake!

## THE HAYES STUPPY STORY

ABOVE: Hayes Stuppy and his father.

The octopus hovered motionless, a glinting black eye fixed on the wiffle golf ball. Suddenly, a tentacle shot out and wrapped around it, jerking the ball to the bottom of the aquarium.

"Did you see how fast that was?" crowed twelve-year-old Hayes Stuppy. He was bent over the aquarium with one hand in the water up to his elbow, his brown hair swinging forward into his eyes. "He throws his tentacles like a lasso, like Indiana Jones."

"That's cool," said Sam. Sam, also twelve, was a flaming redhead.

"Now watch this." Hayes gently wiggled his fingers in the water. After a moment, the octopus snaked an arm up and tossed the wiffle ball back to him. Hayes caught it and pulled it up, dripping, from the water.

"See? He plays catch," he said. "He's really smart. And sneaky."

"Sneaky? How?"

"He's an escape artist. Watch." Putting the ball

aside, Hayes plunged his hand back into the water and pretended to move the rocks around on the bottom. Without warning, the fist-sized octopus shot over and wrapped itself around his hand—then started crawling up his arm!

Sam made a face. "Is it grabbing your arm with its suckers?"

Hayes was busy trying to pry the octopus loose. "Yeah. And you wouldn't believe how strong he is." He pried one slimy green tentacle loose, but there were still seven to go. "My dad was playing with him the other day, and the octopus wrapped his hand. My dad's pretty strong, but this guy *forced* his fingers apart."

Hayes pulled another tentacle loose, but the octopus promptly wrapped the first one around him again. Maybe this hadn't been such a great idea.

"It looks really slimy," Sam said.

"It's about the slimiest, ickiest thing in the world," Hayes said. "My dad says it's slimier than anything he has to touch at work. And you know with *his* work, that's pretty bad!"

Hayes's father was a doctor who specialized in diseases of the stomach and intestines. "Gross," said Sam with feeling. "Can I touch it?"

"Sure."

Sam tried to sneak up on it from behind, but the octopus saw him coming and lashed out with a tentacle. Startled, Sam jerked his hand back.

Hayes laughed. "He's not gonna hurt you."

Sam looked doubtful, but tried again. He used one finger to lightly pet the top of the octopus' rounded head. It felt like snot. He wiped his finger briskly on his T-shirt. "Cool. How long do octopuses live?"

"About a year. Our last one keeled after just a few months, though. My dad put him in a jar of formalin." He pried the last tentacle loose and shook the creature off into the water. "I need to feed him. You want to watch?"

"Sure!"

Hayes grabbed a small fish net. "We have to go out to the living room and snag some guppies."

The octopus tank was in Dr. and Mrs. Stuppy's third-floor bedroom. The Stuppys' house in Los Angeles, California, looked like a real-life castle. It had three stories,  ten or eleven bedrooms, and lots of balconies and fireplaces everywhere. It even had a round turret sticking up from the roof! The top floor

ABOVE: The Stuppy house, Hayes and his family live on the third floor.

had its own living room, kitchen, and dining room. The family lived on the third floor, except when they had company.

The eighty-gallon guppy tank was in the living room. The tank was filled with dozens of colorful tropical fish of all sizes. A huge "kissing fish" glided past the glass, its fish lips puckered. Hayes scooped up two guppies and carried them, dripping, across the carpet and back into his parents' bedroom.

"Hayes! Whatcha doing?" Five-year-old Ben had spotted them on their way down the hall. He was the youngest Stuppy, a freckled redhead with bright green eyes. He looked up to Hayes and tried to imitate him. Hayes liked him.

"We're feeding the octopus," Hayes answered. "Want to watch?"

"Yeah!"

Hayes walked over to the octopus tank. "Watch this," he said, dumping the guppies into the water.

The confused guppies darted back and forth, attracting the octopus' eye. He grew still and settled closer to the bottom. As the three boys watched, a tentacle shot out and circled one of the guppies. In the blink of an eye, the fish disappeared into the octopus' beak-like mouth.

Sam stared in fascination. "He ate that guppy like he was popping an olive into his mouth."

Hayes smiled. "He's a lot of fun. He's a lot smarter than our dog, that's for sure."

Ben giggled. "Beck-y!" he called, clapping his hands. "C'mere, girl!"

Rebecca was their Yorkshire terrier. She was small, furry, and not too bright. She came bouncing in, her pink tongue hanging out. Ben picked her up and buried his face in her fur. "I don't think she's that dumb," he said, his voice muffled.

Behind them, Dr. Stuppy's voice suddenly boomed out: "What are you doing?" Hayes, Sam, and Ben all jumped and spun around. The bedroom behind them was empty except for two large African parrot cages. Hayes rolled his eyes and walked over to the cage in one corner. A silver-gray parrot with a bright red tail sat innocently on a perch inside.

"Knock it off, Sammie!" he said. Max, another African parrot, watched from his cage across the room. They were Mrs. Stuppy's pets. Max didn't talk, but Sammie could imitate voices, bark like a dog, and even ring like the telephone.

The parrot tilted her head sideways and fixed a bright eye on Hayes. "How are you?" she purred, in Mrs. Stuppy's voice.

"Hungry," Hayes told her nastily. "Maybe for some fried parrot!"

The bird barked at him, then added sweetly, "Get out of here!"

Sam burst into laughter. "You guys have some strange pets. I love coming here. It's never boring!"

Hayes smiled. It was true. His house was never boring. Besides the family octopus, Becky, Sammie, and Max, they had a cockatiel named Claire, a parakeet that belonged to his sister, and fish tanks in almost every bedroom. That wasn't counting the two or three "pickled" octopuses his dad had saved in jars after they died. For some reason, he liked keeping dead things in jars.

"Hey, you want a Dr Pepper?" Hayes asked.

"Sounds good." As the boys walked from the bedroom, the parrot began to ring: "Brrr-rring! Brrr-rring!" Hayes didn't go back to answer her.

Ben tagged along as they walked through the living room and into the kitchen. Hayes poured two big glasses of Dr Pepper for himself and Sam, and a little glass for Ben.

"Don't spill it," he warned as he handed Ben the drink.

"I won't." Holding the glass carefully, Ben headed for the TV room. It was Friday afternoon, and cartoons were on.

"Hey, where are your sisters?" Sam asked. "It's quiet here today. Did you lock Jaime in a closet or something?"

Hayes laughed. "I wish. I think she's spending the weekend at her friend Emily's house. I don't know where Meggie is."

Jaime was ten and had long brown-blond hair; Meggie was eight with red hair and freckles. Hayes got along okay with Meggie, but Jaime drove him crazy. They were always arguing.

They were walking back through the living room heading for the hall when Dr. Stuppy came out of his office. "What are you two doing?" he asked, sounding just like the parrot. Hayes and Sam both laughed.

Hayes held up his Dr Pepper. "Getting drinks."

Sam waved. "Hi, Dr. Stuppy."

Dr. Stuppy was tall with graying brown hair, keen blue eyes, and a thick mustache that slid around the sides of his mouth into a small beard. Unlike many of his doctor friends, he was in good shape. Best of all, he didn't act like a dork around Hayes's friends.

"Hi, Sam," Dr. Stuppy replied. "You getting ready for all the bike training coming up?"

Sam and Hayes were both in Boy Scout Troop #621. The troop was planning a big European bicycle trip for the following summer. Training was scheduled to start in a few weeks. Dr. Stuppy had volunteered to help out by doing the troop's medical exams.

"I think so," Sam replied. "We're riding bikes to the L.A. Zoo at the end of the month. After that, we'll be taking trips every other weekend."

"Sounds like fun."

Hayes nodded. "I can't wait to go to San Diego. We get to ride all the way down there and take the train back."

Dr. Stuppy smiled. "That reminds me—I'm supposed to teach first aid at your next troop meeting. Everybody who wants to do the San Diego trip has to have their First Aid Merit Badge."

"Uh-huh." Hayes glanced around the upstairs. It *was* uncommonly quiet. "Where's Mom? I want to see if Sam can spend the night."

"She's around someplace." Dr. Stuppy waved his hand in the air vaguely. In a house the size of the Stuppys', it was easy to misplace people. "Come to think of it, she might've taken Meggie somewhere."

Hayes decided to take advantage of his mother's absence. "Can we order pizza tonight?"

"Good idea. Could you boys call it in? You know what kind of toppings everybody likes."

"Sure," Hayes said. "Oh, by the way . . . you don't have to work or anything tonight, do you?"

Dr. Stuppy sometimes got called in for emergencies at the Hospital of the Good Samaritan, nicknamed "Good Sam's" around their house. It didn't happen often, but Hayes always felt sorry for his dad when he had to work nights. His father didn't seem to mind, though. He liked being a doctor.

"Not tonight," Dr. Stuppy said cheerfully. "Why?"

Hayes grinned sheepishly. "Well, I was wondering if you'd drop us off at the mall or the movies."

"I thought you had something in mind. I guess I could do that."

"Thanks, Dad." Hayes nudged Sam. "C'mon, let's

go order the pizza. While we're waiting, we can eat some candy that I've got stashed in my room. That is, unless Jaime took it again. If she did, she'd better just stay at Emily's."

The whole family had bedrooms on the third floor. Hayes's room was near the top of the stairs, between his parents' room and his brother's and sisters' rooms. He went over to his dresser to check on his candy. It was still there.

"What do you want?" he asked Sam, stirring a small collection of red Twizzlers, jawbreakers, Butterfingers, and Hot Tamales.

"Twizzlers. And maybe one jawbreaker."

Hayes tossed the candy to Sam, then fished out a Butterfinger bar for himself. He peeled the wrapper off like a banana and took a big bite.

"Mmm," he said. "I was hungry." He washed it down with a swig of Dr Pepper and belched happily.

Sam wandered over to look at the tall trophy case in the corner. Hayes had played soccer and baseball for years, so the shelves were lined with plaques and trophies. The latest soccer season had just ended a few weeks before.

"You've won a lot of stuff," Sam said indistinctly, a jawbreaker bulging in one cheek.

Hayes licked chocolate off his fingers. "They give you plaques a lot of times just for playing. Even if you stink."

Sam snickered. "Do you stink?"

"Are you kidding? I'm the best center halfback on the team!" He bit off another hunk of Butterfinger. "I hope that pizza gets here soon. I'm starving."

"Blood is spurting from a nasty wound. What do you do?"

"Run!" a voice murmured. Dr. Stuppy smiled as a wave of giggles started across the room. He was at the Tuesday night meeting of Boy Scout Troop #621. Hayes and Sam were sitting together in the back.

A hand went up, and Dr. Stuppy nodded encouragement. "Yes?"

"You apply pressure?" the boy suggested uncertainly.

"That's right. You can't be timid just because so much blood is coming out." He paused to let another wave of nervous giggles die down. "You have to find the source and apply pressure. I'm going to show you how to do that. Can I get a volunteer?"

This time hands shot up all over the room. Dr. Stuppy picked one of the younger boys.

"Okay," he said, patting his victim's shoulder. "Let's say this young man was just in a car wreck. He's got a deep gash right here"—he lifted the boy's right arm and drew his finger in a jagged line across the upper part of it—"and it's bleeding badly. Get your Scout handbooks out so you can follow along."

"Should I lie down?" the boy asked.

"Certainly." Dr. Stuppy waited until the young

Scout was stretched out on the floor, then knelt beside him. "Okay, here we go. With an arm or leg, the first thing you want to do is raise the injured part above body level." He gently lifted the boy's right arm to demonstrate. "That helps control the bleeding."

The boys all leaned forward to see. The "victim" smiled and waggled his fingers at them, happy to be the center of attention.

"If a wound is actually spurting blood—pumping it out in big spurts—it means an artery has been cut. Arteries are big blood vessels that carry blood from the heart out into the body. If you cut an artery, you can bleed to death very quickly."

The boys stared down at their handbooks with interest. A drawing showed the arteries in arms and legs.

Dr. Stuppy continued, "Most bleeding, even arterial bleeding, can be stopped by direct pressure. You need a cloth pad of some kind . . . a bandanna, shirt, or any other clean cloth will do in an emergency. You cover the wound like this"—he laid a cloth pad over his victim's imaginary cut—"and press *hard*."

The boy on the floor looked surprised. "You're really squashing my arm."

Dr. Stuppy nodded. "You have to press hard or it doesn't work. If the edges of the wound are gaping open, you should try to hold them together. And whatever you do, *don't* remove the pad to check on the wound. You'll just break the blood clot that's forming."

The room suddenly grew still. In the back, Hayes hid a smile. He was used to hearing about gaping wounds and blood clots, but a lot of the other boys weren't. His father had their undivided attention.

Dr. Stuppy didn't notice the sudden silence. "If you've got a cut artery, sometimes just pressure won't work. In those cases you have to pinch off an artery temporarily, sort of like stepping on a water hose. You do that by pressing the artery against a nearby bone. The pictures in your book show the spots where that works best."

Continuing to press down on the cloth pad with one hand, Dr. Stuppy held up a bandage roll with the other. "After you press a pad over a wound, you should wrap it with a bandage to hold it in place. You can use a real bandage like this if you have one, or make a 'cravat bandage' with a bandanna or neckerchief."

Sam studied the pictures in his book. They showed a boy folding the point of a large triangle-shaped cloth up to the long edge, then folding it up twice more to make a long, skinny bandage.

"Easy," he whispered to Hayes. Hayes didn't bother to look. He had already earned his First Aid Merit Badge, so this was all just a review for him.

"If blood soaks through the pad and bandage, *don't take it off*. Just add another pad and bandage on top of it and keep pressing."

Dr. Stuppy stood up slowly, his joints popping. He

helped his young victim up before asking, "Any questions?"

One of the older boys raised his hand. "What about head wounds? Do you treat them the same way?"

"Only with a minor cut. With serious head injuries, you should never try to move the person or press hard on the wound. You can accidentally press bone splinters into the brain."

Brain splinters. If his dad hadn't been there, Hayes might have been tempted to make a smart remark. He could think of several people in the troop who *acted* like they had brain splinters.

"Okay, why don't you all pick a partner and practice?" Dr. Stuppy suggested. "You can take turns being the victim."

Sam looked over at Hayes. "Can I practice on you?"

"Sure. Where should I be cut?"

Sam grinned evilly. "Across your throat?"

"I don't think so. How about my little finger?" Hayes waggled his pinkie in the air.

"Forget that. Okay, I've got it. You've got a little head wound. Now lie down and be quiet."

Hayes flopped back and lay still. "Oh-hh-hh," he moaned faintly. "I think I'm dying. Everything's getting black . . ."

"Maybe I should start by bandaging your mouth."

Hayes grinned and fell silent. He watched through slitted eyes as Sam wrapped his head. He felt like a tree being toilet-papered. Finally, Sam sat back to admire his work.

"Well? How does that feel?"

Hayes sat up and gently touched the bandages. "Er . . . if I ever need something bandaged just call my dad, okay?"

"Like you could do better," Sam retorted.

Later, on the way home, Hayes was unusually talkative. "You know, Dad, I've been thinking. I don't want to work on people like you do, but I think it might be fun to work with animals. Do surgeries and stuff like that."

Dr. Stuppy nodded. "You've always been good with animals. You'd probably make a good veterinarian." He laughed. "We have enough animals around the house for you to practice on."

When they got home, Jaime was the only one downstairs. She was in the big-screen TV room watching a movie.

"Hi, honey!" Dr. Stuppy called on his way to the stairs. "What are you watching?"

"*The Little Mermaid*. Nobody else wanted to watch it, so I came down here." She sounded sulky.

Hayes lowered his voice. "She's only watched it about fifty times. Even Ben is tired of it."

"I heard you, Hayes!" Jaime said. "Why don't you just be quiet?"

Dr. Stuppy shook his head and started upstairs. He usually stayed out of arguments. Hayes thought about saying something back to Jaime, but decided it wasn't worth the effort. It was a long climb to the third floor. He needed to save his energy.

The whole second floor was used by Kane ("Kahnee") and Tutu, Dr. Stuppy's parents. Hayes didn't see much of them except for the times when they all ate dinner together downstairs. Before coming to California, his grandfather had been stationed in Hawaii. Kane and Tutu were the Hawaiian names for grandfather and grandmother.

By the time Hayes reached the third floor, he was out of breath. He had often wished their house had an elevator, especially after hard soccer or baseball games. His parents insisted the exercise was good for him. He wasn't so sure.

He had just walked into his room when he heard his mother calling. At least he *thought* it was his mother. Sammie had fooled him more than once by imitating her voice.

"Mom?" He went to his parents' room, sidestepping the large empty aquarium that stood outside in the hall. It wasn't the octopus tank; so far they'd kept him out of Dr. Stuppy's dead-things-in-jars collection. It was an extra aquarium that they were moving from one room to another.

Mrs. Stuppy smiled when he walked in. "Hi, honey. How was Boy Scouts?" She was the same height as Hayes, with short brown hair and brown eyes.

"Fine. Dad did his first aid thing, and I let Sam bandage my head."

In the corner, Sammie started bobbing her head up and down irritably, trying to get Mrs. Stuppy's attention. They both ignored her.

"So your dad did well?"

"Sure. The guys all think he's cool."

Sammie was practically rocking her cage back and forth. "Get out *now!*" she shrieked at Hayes.

"Settle down, Sammie," Mrs. Stuppy scolded. "I'll come talk to you in a minute. You're so spoiled!"

The bird sulked in silence as Hayes told his mom about Sam's first aid attempts. Finally, he excused himself.

"I need to go finish my homework," he explained. "I didn't have time before Boy Scouts."

"All right. Do you know where your dad is?"

Hayes waved his hand in the air vaguely. "He's here somewhere." They were always losing people around the house.

Several weeks passed. Between school, Boy Scouts, and friends, Hayes stayed busy. He liked the middle of January because it fell between soccer and baseball seasons. He planned to take advantage of his freedom while it lasted.

As usual, he spent Sunday afternoon over at Sam's house. He came home around five o'clock hoping for dinner. After trudging all the way upstairs, he found his mom sitting in the living room instead of the kitchen—not a good sign. He sniffed the air hopefully for lasagna or roast beef smells. The air was sadly foodless.

"When's dinner?" he asked. "I mean, hi Mom. When's dinner?"

Mrs. Stuppy raised an eyebrow. "Hi, Hayes. Nice to see you. We'll be eating a little later than usual tonight. Your dad got called in on an emergency this afternoon, but he should be home soon."

Hayes's stomach gurgled. "Oh." If dinner was going to be late, he needed a candy bar to give him strength. He headed toward his room.

The empty aquarium was still sitting in the hall. Hayes glanced at it idly, wondering if his parents were ever going to move it out of the way. It was a road hazard.

He grabbed some Hot Tamales off his dresser and flopped back on his bed. As he munched the candy, his eyes drifted across the ceiling to the attic entrance, a square wooden door built into the ceiling. If you pulled it open, a ladder unfolded from the ceiling. He could climb straight up from his room into the attic.

*I ought to make a secret hangout up there sometime,* he thought. *I could sneak a couple of chairs up, and maybe a little TV. I could hide up there and nobody would find me.*

Of course, considering how hard it was already to find people in their house, what was the point? He decided that making a secret hiding place sounded like too much work. Maybe some other time.

He glanced over at the tall trophy case in the corner, admiring his newest soccer trophy. It was on the top shelf wedged in between two plaques. His team had done well this season.

"Hayes! Dad's home and Mom says it's almost time for dinner." Hayes looked up just in time to catch a glimpse of Meggie's red hair flashing away down the hall. On his way out, he scrunched up his Hot Tamales box and tossed it into the trash. He had to get rid of the evidence before his mom caught him snacking before dinner.

Dr. Stuppy was sitting at the dining room table. He looked tired. Hayes sat down across from him.

"Hi, Dad."

"Hi, son. How was your day?"

"Fine." Hayes had learned not to ask about his father's day. Once he got started, he could talk about intestines and diseases like they were the most interesting things in the world.

Mrs. Stuppy had made tacos and rice. "Jaime, will you set the food out on the counter? Meggie, you can pour drinks." She glanced over the counter before adding, "Hayes, go find your brother and tell him it's dinnertime."

Ben wouldn't be in the TV room; on Sunday nights they had a "No TV" rule. He wasn't in the living room, so unless he was somewhere else in the house, he must be playing back in his room. Maybe. Hayes walked to the end of the hallway and yelled, "Ben! Dinner!"

The little boy popped out of his room down the hall.

"I'm coming!" he called. Hayes waited for him, and they walked back to the dining room together.

They all ate quickly, not talking much. When the last taco was gone, Dr. Stuppy scooted his chair back. "Well, I guess it's time for Family Council. Let's get on with it while I'm still awake. It's been a long day."

They had started the Family Councils a few years before. Every Sunday night, they all gathered in the living room to discuss plans for the following week. It kept things from getting too confused. School events, soccer games, dance lessons, T-ball practice, sleep-overs . . . Dr. and Mrs. Stuppy went around the room to make sure each kid's schedule was worked out.

At the end, Dr. Stuppy handed out allowances. That was the kids' favorite part.

The only thing Hayes had going was his usual Tuesday night Boy Scout meeting. Jaime, Meggie, and Ben didn't have much to do, either. It was going to be a dull week.

"Anything else we need to talk about?" Dr. Stuppy asked. "Problems? Old business?"

"No!" the kids all chorused. With a smile, Dr. Stuppy pulled out his wallet. Allowance time at last!

When it was his turn, Hayes pocketed his allowance carefully. He couldn't wait until he was old enough to get a real job. Once he could earn his own money, he wouldn't need an allowance.

After the Sunday night Family Councils, Hayes usually went to bed early. With no TV to watch, there wasn't much else to do. He was beginning to suspect that his parents planned it that way. They bored everybody into an early bedtime.

He brushed his teeth, went to his room, and closed the door. Kicking off his jeans, he threw them across the back of a chair before clicking on his small radio. He fell asleep most nights listening to his favorite station. He could always tell when his dad had checked on him at night, because in the morning his radio would be turned off.

With a yawn, Hayes turned off the light and slipped under the covers. He slept in boxers and a T-shirt, even in the middle of the winter. Of course, in Los Angeles, winter wasn't all that different from summer.

He closed his eyes and drifted off, half-listening to the tinkling music on the radio.

A violent, musical clanging jolted Hayes from a deep sleep. He blinked and peered groggily at his clock. It was 4:33 A.M.

It took him a few seconds to realize the noise was coming from the wind chimes hanging on the third-floor balcony. Suddenly Hayes was wide awake. The three or four other times he'd been jolted from sleep by the chimes had been during earthquakes.

*An earthquake.* Every nerve tingling, Hayes felt the house beneath him begin to sway gently: The floor creaked and popped as the chimes outside crashed and clanged even louder.

"Cool," Hayes whispered. He had always thought that earthquakes were kind of exciting. Sometimes they made stuff slide off tables or jumbled dishes in the kitchen cabinets, but few did any real damage. He decided to stay in bed and wait for this one to pass.

He lay there for about thirty seconds, eyes wide in the darkness. The wind chimes clanged angrily as the swaying motion increased. A rumbling noise grew louder and louder. For the first time, Hayes felt uneasy. This one was lasting a long time!

He was wondering if he should get up when the heavy trophy case in the corner suddenly pulled away from the wall. It toppled into the room with a grinding crash, scattering his plaques and trophies across his carpet.

Hayes shot out of bed, his heart pounding. His room felt like the deck of a ship, swaying back and forth. All around, he could hear things crashing and breaking. It sounded like the house was being pulled apart.

He headed for the door.

He ran out into the hallway wearing only his boxers and a T-shirt. The whole upstairs was pitch black. Loud creaks and crashes echoed up the long staircase. The rumbles were now a thunderous roar that vibrated through his body, like being in the middle of heavy bass drums. There was noise from every direction, and over it all, the wind chimes.

Hayes froze, trying to get his bearings. In the dark confusion, nothing looked familiar.

The electricity must be out, he thought. I've got to get Mom and Dad. They'll know what to do. Wheeling to the right, Hayes stumbled toward his parents' room.

Dr. Stuppy was sound asleep until the crash from Hayes's room woke him. It woke Mrs. Stuppy at the same time. As soon as they opened their eyes, they knew they were in trouble.

It was an earthquake, and a big one.

"The kids!" Mrs. Stuppy shouted, scrambling out of bed. Dr. Stuppy clawed his way out of bed on the other side. Together, they ran for the door.

They collided in the doorway, then ran out into the dark hall. All the kids' bedrooms were to their left. Dr. Stuppy, barefoot and in a bathrobe, led the way.

They had only taken a few steps when Dr. Stuppy's left ankle slammed into what felt like saw blades. The empty tank in the hall had fallen and shattered, leaving a nightmare of knife-like glass shards. Dr. Stuppy pitched forward onto it, and his wife fell on top of him. They both jumped up and kept going.

In the blackness, neither of them could see the trail of dark blood they had left behind.

Hayes heard his parents' voices just ahead. "Mom! Dad!"

His father's shadowy figure loomed in front of him. "Go stand in our bedroom doorway. We're getting the other kids. *Go!*"

Hayes nodded. His parents ran past him. His eyes had adjusted to the darkness enough to see the broken aquarium on the floor. He edged around it. The house was still shaking and swaying. The noise was almost unbearable. Reaching his parents' doorway, he grabbed it and held on.

Hayes's heart beat wildly as he took it all in. It seemed unreal. Living in southern California, everybody sort of took earthquakes for granted. They had drills at school and sold "survival kits" in grocery stores, but the earthquakes that usually hit were no big deal.

Now Hayes tried to remember what you were supposed to do in a big earthquake. Stand in an inside doorway . . . stay away from windows . . . stay away from heavy things that could fall. But what if your *house* fell down?

The whole top floor was swaying like a tree branch in a storm.

His parents came running back. His mom was carrying Ben, and his dad had Meggie and Jaime. "Downstairs," Dr. Stuppy said shortly. "We need to make sure Kane and Tutu are safe."

His grandparents! Hayes had forgotten all about them. He fell in behind his mom and dad as they started downstairs. When they reached the second floor, they saw that the elderly couple were already on their way downstairs.

On the first floor, Dr. Stuppy herded everyone into the kitchen. They kept flashlights and a battery radio there for emergencies. Tutu snapped the radio on.

"Okay, everybody get under doorways!" Mrs. Stuppy ordered. "Hayes, you hang on to Ben. Meggie, Jaime, you come over here with me."

Dr. Stuppy suddenly slapped his forehead. "Holy smoke! What about all the animals? I've got to go check on them."

Jaime's eyes widened. "Becky!" The Yorkshire terrier hadn't followed them downstairs.

"I'll go with you," Mrs. Stuppy told her husband. "Kids, you stay down here with Kane and Tutu. We'll be right back." They each grabbed a flashlight and ran for the stairs.

Hayes wanted to go along, but he knew they'd say no. He hoped they'd find Becky. The little dog slept in a different bedroom almost every night. He was surprised she hadn't come out when they were all running up and down the hallway.

Hayes got out another flashlight and flashed it around the kitchen. Drawers had fallen out onto the floor, and glasses had shattered on the counters. It was a mess. And it wasn't over yet. The house was still shaking and vibrating.

Then he saw something dark and wet smeared across the kitchen floor. He followed the marks with his flashlight out onto the gold carpet. It looked like bloody footprints.

The radio announcer's voice filled the kitchen:

*"Minutes ago, an earthquake measuring 6.7 on the Richter scale hit Los Angeles and Ventura counties. As aftershocks continue, reports of widespread damage are pouring in from the Northridge–San Fernando area. . . ."*

Hayes was stunned. This *was* a big one! Where were his mom and dad?

Mrs. Stuppy hurried back into the kitchen just then with Becky at her heels. Jaime clapped her hands and the little dog ran over to her, tail wagging.

"Are your birds okay?" Hayes asked.

Mrs. Stuppy shrugged tiredly. "Max is fine, but I think Sammie is hurt. There's blood all over the wall behind her cage, but it might just be because she's pulling out her feathers. Parrots sometimes do that when they're really upset."

Her words reminded Hayes. "Somebody's tracking blood all over the carpet. See?" He pointed his light at the gold carpet outside the kitchen.

Mrs. Stuppy looked down at her feet. "It must be your father. We both ran into the tank in the dark. I've got some scratches, but he must've really cut himself."

"Where is he?"

"He's still upstairs."

Hayes idly shined his flashlight toward the stairs—then froze. In the flashlight beam, a dark trail of blood was clearly visible leading up the gold-carpeted stairs.

"I'm going up to check on him," Hayes said. "I'll be right back."

"Wait! I'll come with you."

Aftershocks were still rumbling through the house as they raced up the bloodstained stairs. At the top, Hayes flashed his light in a big circle. "Dad?"

"William?" Mrs. Stuppy called. "Where are you?"

Dr. Stuppy didn't answer. But as they strained their ears, they both heard an odd sound: a low "duh-dump, duh-dump." It sounded like it was coming from the living room.

Mrs. Stuppy shined her light in that direction. The big kissing fish was flopping around on the living room floor. The earthquake must have sloshed him out of the tank.

As Mrs. Stuppy ran over to put the fish back into the aquarium, Hayes stepped into his parents' room. His flashlight instantly picked up a sticky trail of blood. "Dad?" he called. The trail led across the room toward the bathroom. He followed it.

He found his father sitting on the bathroom floor, slumped sideways against the wall. The floor tiles around him were stained with dark puddles of blood.

Hayes ran over to him. "Dad!" he yelled. "Dad!"

Dr. Stuppy didn't answer. Only half-conscious, he slowly lifted his eyes to Hayes's face. Hayes pointed his flashlight down at his father's legs. To his horror, he saw a deep gash running up his left ankle. It was spurting blood with every heartbeat.

*An artery. He had cut an artery.*

With chilling certainty, Hayes knew that unless he did some-thing fast, his father would bleed to death. He looked around wildly. He needed a cloth pad and a bandage! The bathroom towels? They were too big and too thick to tear. The

ABOVE: The bathroom where Hayes found his father.

bathroom rug? No. The upstairs kitchen! He could get paper towels and a small dish towel for a bandage.

"Dad? I'll be right back. Hang on."

Dr. Stuppy was blacking out again. Hayes darted out into the hall and turned right, his stomach churning. He dashed across the living room into the kitchen, his flashlight swinging wildly. His mother was nowhere in sight.

He grabbed the end of the paper-towel roll and yanked, making the roller spin. When he had a big wad of paper towels, he tore them off and grabbed a clean dish towel. He ran back to his father's side.

The smell of the blood puddled around the bathroom made his stomach churn, but his hands stayed steady. "Dad, wake up!" he said sharply. He folded the paper towels into a thick pad and pressed it over the deep gash on his father's ankle.

Dr. Stuppy opened his eyes, but he didn't seem to know what was happening. He had lost a *lot* of blood. Hayes pressed harder on the wad of paper towels. Blood was already soaking up through them.

I need to tie a bandage around his ankle, he thought. It'll help hold the pad tight against the cut. Using his free hand, Hayes snapped the dish towel to straighten it out, then wrapped it around his father's ankle. He tied the towel in a thick knot right over the pad.

Dr. Stuppy groaned. Hayes looked at him in alarm. "Dad? You're going to be all right."

He couldn't tell if his father heard him. Dr. Stuppy reached down with a trembling hand and shifted the knot away from his cut. Was the bandage hurting him? Hayes wasn't sure if he should move it back or not. The knot would help hold the pad tight.

*Maybe I should just tie the bandage tighter,* Hayes thought. He unraveled the knot and retied the towel. This time he knotted it slightly to one side of the wound.

"Dad? Let's get out of here, okay?"

This time Dr. Stuppy seemed to hear him. Hayes looped an arm under his father's arms and helped him to his feet. Dr. Stuppy leaned on him, wobbly and heavy.

"We have to go downstairs now," Hayes said. He had no idea how he was going to get his dad down three long flights of stairs. "Come on."

Dr. Stuppy obeyed, still not fully aware of what was happening. Hayes led him out of the room and into the hall.

"Mom!" he yelled. "Mo-om! We need help. Where are you?"

Mrs. Stuppy was just running up the stairs. "I'm here. I went down to check on the other kids."

"Dad's hurt. Help me get him downstairs."

Mrs. Stuppy didn't stop to ask a million questions. She got on one side of Dr. Stuppy with Hayes on the other. Together, they walked Dr. Stuppy down the endless flights of stairs. When they got to the first floor, they led him to a chair in the kitchen.

Outside, the sky was getting lighter. The radio blared a steady stream of bad news:

*"At least twenty-five people have been reported killed, with thousands more injured. An overpass on the Santa Monica Freeway has collapsed, crushing dozens of motorists and trapping others. Fires are raging in the San Fernando Valley and at Malibu and Venice. Thousands of homes have been destroyed . . ."*

Hayes stared around him. Furniture was tumbled and broken everywhere, but so far the house was still standing. He checked his father's ankle. The bandage was holding. They still needed to get him to the emergency room at Good Sam's, but he was going to survive.

Even if their house fell down later, Hayes didn't care. Houses, even three-story castles, could be replaced. His father couldn't.

*Hayes Stuppy received a National Medal of Heroism from the Boy Scouts of America "for demonstrating heroism and skill" in treating his father's near-fatal wound.*

*It took ten deep sutures to close the gash in Dr. Stuppy's leg. He was treated at the Hospital of the Good Samaritan and released.*

*The earthquake killed at least fifty-six people in southern California and injured more than 7,000. Over 20,000 were left homeless.*

This story was submitted by reader Erin Russell of Austin, Texas.

# A Rope Swing Accident!

## THE AMY TOOLE STORY

ABOVE:  Amy Toole, now age fifteen.

"Over here! C'mon, Heather, I'm clear!" Amy Toole jumped up and down on the dirt road, waving her arms frantically. Heather had the football, but Josh and Bud were about to take it from her. "*Pass it,* Heather!"

The football finally came wobbling through the air toward her. Amy shuffled backward, eyes on the ball. It was just inches from her waiting hands when a train hit her from behind, sending her sprawling facedown into the dirt. The train (whose name was Matthew) snatched the ball and took off with it.

Amy groaned and slowly lifted her head. Her mouth and eyes were full of dirt. She spat, then made a face. She'd never liked the taste of dirt, especially the kind in roads. Matthew was going to pay for this!

Josh and Jason, the two homeschoolers who lived at the end of the street, puffed up to her. "Hey, are you okay?" Josh asked, offering a hand to help her up.

"Heck, yeah," she said defiantly, ignoring his hand. She leaped up to brush the dirt off her clothes. "But Matthew had better stop tackling people. We're supposed to be playing touch."

Josh and Jason looked at each other. "Er, he didn't really *tackle* you, Amy," Jason said apologetically. "He just kind of accidentally ran over you."

"Uh-huh. Did you let him score?"

"Yeah. Well, we didn't *let* him score, but he did."

Amy scowled. At age twelve, she was good at football, one of the best players in the neighborhood. She hated to lose. "Okay, time-out," she said. "Let's get Ashley and Heather over here so we can plan our next play." She added, green eyes flashing, "Maybe we should all 'accidentally' run over Matthew . . . and my little brother, while we're at it!"

The small neighborhood in Royal Palm Beach, Florida, was all dirt roads and trees and horses. Amy liked it. She lived in a ranch-style house with her parents and two younger brothers, Bud and Bryan. Bud was ten, and Bryan was five. They both liked playing street football, but Bryan usually ended up getting trampled. Now Amy knew what he felt like.

In late August the air was hot and sticky. School would be starting in less than a week. Amy was excited about moving up to Royal Pines School. Bud still had a couple more years to go to Acreage Pines Elementary.

In the meantime, Amy had a football game to win.

Shaking the dirt from her curly brown hair, she motioned to the other team that they were ready to play.

Thirty minutes later, sweaty, dirty, and flushed with victory, Amy trotted into the house. She found Bryan watching TV. "My team won!" she announced. "We beat Bud's team!"

Bryan jumped up with a big grin, his dark eyes sparkling behind his glasses. "Yay!!" he cheered.

Amy grinned down at him. "Thanks. And look at this!" She showed him her skinned elbows and knees. "Matthew ran right over me. I was roadkill!"

Bryan's small face grew concerned. "Ooh, does that hurt? I'll go get you a Band-Aid. Stay right there!"

Before she could reply, he scampered off down the hall toward the bathroom. Amy smiled to herself. She was usually the one bandaging *his* cuts and scrapes. She guessed that he wanted to be the bandager for a change.

Bryan bounced back into the room a moment later grasping a handful of slightly squashed Band-Aids. "Okay," he told Amy sternly, "I'm going to stick these on for you. Just hold still."

"Yes, sir." Amy meekly held out her elbows, then watched in amusement as Bryan stuck a crisscross of Band-Aids over her bloody elbows and knees.

"There!" he finally said, pleased with his work. "Does that feel better?"

"Absolutely. Thanks, Bryan." Amy gave him a quick squeeze, which left his glasses tilted sideways on his face. She was careful not to let any of the Band-Aids fall off when she stood up. Bryan would want to pull them off and start all over again.

Shuffling down the hall toward her room like a stiff-legged mummy, Amy thought fondly of the day Bryan was born. She and Bud had gone to their mom's hospital room to meet their new baby brother. To Amy's seven-year-old eyes, he had looked like a little doll. She couldn't remember anything about Bud's birth. Considering how he'd turned out, though, he had probably started pestering the other newborns the minute he got to the nursery!

"Brothers!" she said to herself, half-smiling, as she shuffled into her room and started prying Band-Aids loose.

Heather Davis was tall and thin, with red-brown hair and a sprinkle of freckles across her nose. She smiled when she saw Amy on her front step, a lumpy pillow smashed under one arm. A nightgown sleeve dangled out of the pillowcase.

"Hi! Are you ready for me, yet?" Amy asked.

"Sure. Mom! Amy's here!" Heather motioned for her to come in. "We just finished dinner, but tonight's my sister's night to do the dishes. You feel like going riding for a little while?"

"You bet! Just let me throw my overnight stuff in your room."

It was Thursday night Amy and Heather had decided to spend one of their last free weeknights at Heather's house. They planned to stay up really late to make up for all the early bedtimes to come once school started.

Heather's horse, Cindy, was a brown and black quarter horse. Since Heather's mother was also named Cindy, a lot of people teased her about it. Heather always had to explain that the horse was already named when they had gotten her. Besides, Cindy-the-horse's full name was "Cindy Sue."

Amy had never ridden a horse until she had moved across the street from Heather the year before. She still didn't like riding by herself, but it was fun riding doubles. The girls were both light, so Cindy Sue didn't mind.

Amy followed Heather out to the stable and watched her friend quickly brush down the horse, then sling a pad and saddle over her back. Cindy Sue stood quietly, rolling her eyes as Heather yanked the girth strap tight.

"Sometimes she puffs up and holds her breath when you're saddling her," Heather explained. "If you don't pull the strap really tight, the whole saddle can slide sideways when she lets out her breath."

Amy laughed. "Smart-aleck horse."

Heather fit the bridle over the horse's head and slid the metal bit between its teeth. Cindy Sue wiggled her lips up and down and chewed the bit a few times, like she was tasting it. Finally, Heather swung herself up into the saddle.

"Okay, come on up," she said. Amy scrambled up behind her. Heather loosened the reins and made a clicking sound with her tongue. Cindy Sue gave a big, horse sigh and started walking.

"Where do you want to go?" Heather asked, squinting against the sun. They were heading for the dirt road.

"I dunno. Just up and down the street, I guess." Amy wasn't crazy about being on the back of Heather's horse when it trotted or galloped. Since she didn't have stirrups for her feet, she just had to hang on to Heather. It got pretty bouncy sometimes.

Heather steered the horse onto the edge of the dirt road, pointing it in the direction of Josh and Jason's house. There were several fields with other horses along the way, and Cindy Sue paused to whinny at several of them. Amy wondered idly what it might mean in horse talk. "Hi there"? "You look stupid"? "My back hurts"?

"I wonder what teachers I'm going to get this year," Heather said, interrupting Amy's thoughts. "I can't believe it's already time for school to start."

"Me neither. But at least I'm not going back to Acreage Elementary like you. It'll be nice to get away from all the little kids."

"Yeah . . ." At the end of the road, Heather pulled the reins over to one side, and the horse obediently made a U-turn. "At least this year I won't be in the youngest grade anymore. I hate that."

The sun was dipping below the trees as they started back. It was a relief; sitting on a hot, sweaty horse in the blazing sun wasn't very comfortable. It didn't smell that great, either. Amy looked down at her shorts. They looked kind of dirty and smelled like horse.

Back at Heather's house they stalled the horse, unsaddled it, and went inside. The air-conditioning felt wonderful! Amy followed Heather's example by plopping down on the couch, sweaty shorts and all. If Heather's mom didn't mind, Amy didn't either.

"So, what do you want to do tonight?" Heather asked, stifling a yawn.

"Not sleep, that's for sure. Stop yawning! This is our last free weeknight, remember?"

"Um-hm. You want to watch TV?"

Well, *there* was an original idea. But after a moment's thought, Amy couldn't come up with a better one. She shrugged. "Okay."

They decided to go back to Heather's room. The TV was smaller than the one in the living room, but at least that way Heather's little sister, Holli, wouldn't be bothering them the whole time.

Heather turned on her TV, then dragged the comforter off her bed. "Want to just sleep on the floor?" she asked, spreading the comforter out in front of the TV. "There's a lot more room."

"Fine with me." Amy tossed her pillow onto the floor and flopped down next to Heather. Lying on their stomachs, pillows bunched up under their arms, the two girls glanced up at the TV. It was all commercials.

"I think I'll study for my catechism during commercials," Heather said. "I'm going to be confirmed in a couple of weeks." The "catechism" is a kind of test to make sure people understand the basics of what the Catholic Church believes.

"Want me to ask you questions or anything?" Amy offered.

"Maybe in a minute. This part is pretty easy. It's about not committing murder."

Amy snorted. "Right. Like you'd go, 'Oops! I forgot I wasn't supposed to kill anybody.' "

They both looked up when a *Rescue 9-1-1* commercial came on. William Shatner appeared on the screen. In a dramatic voice he said:

"*A woman home alone hears an intruder in her basement and calls 9-1-1, then stays on the line as the man passes within inches of where she's hiding . . .*"

Amy laughed. "Doesn't William Shatner look funny in a suit? I liked him better as Captain Kirk . . . 'BOLDLY GOING WHERE NO MAN HAS GONE BEFORE!!!' "

"He's pretty old now," Heather said. "He'd probably look dumb in his Star Trek suit." She studied the actor critically. "I'll bet he dyes his hair."

"Maybe it's a wig. And it looks like he's had a permanent, too. His hair didn't used to be curly, did it?"

"Nope. He probably has false teeth, too." Heather was getting into the spirit. "And plastic surgery."

"Yeah. All actors have plastic surgery. They'll be like eighty years old and still try to look like they're twenty. It's dumb."

William Shatner, happily unaware of their comments, was going on: *"An eleven-year-old girl, a recent graduate of a Red Cross class, sprints into action when she finds her three-year-old brother floating facedown in a swimming pool . . ."*

Amy made a face. "I hate stories like that. It always makes me think about something happening to Bryan."

"I already saw that one," Heather said. "This girl was playing in a pool with some friends or something when her little brother fell in. They didn't see him at first. When the girl saw her brother floating facedown she freaked out. She pulled him out and did CPR until he started breathing again."

"Wow," Amy said, impressed. "That would be so cool to know. I mean, how to do CPR and stuff."

Heather shrugged. "I know how. They taught us CPR in Health class last year. It isn't so hard."

"Really? I'd love to know how to do it just in case something bad ever happens. Could you teach me?"

"If you want." Heather looked around the room. "You're supposed to use a CPR dummy. That was the part I hated at school. They made us get up in front of the whole class and work on this dummy. It looked like we were kissing it. Everybody laughed at you the whole time." She glanced around the room. "I guess we could use a pillow or something instead."

Amy thrust her pillow toward her friend. "Here, use mine. Now what do you do?"

Frowning with concentration, Heather laid the pillow down between them. She fluffed it a few times, then grabbed it around its "throat" and squeezed, trying to squash the pillow into a head-and-body shape.

Amy started laughing. "You're strangling the poor thing! I thought you were trying to save it, not kill it."

"I was trying to make it look more like a person," Heather retorted. "Most people have heads on top of their bodies."

"Yeah . . . Maybe that's what's wrong with my brother. Bud was born without a head."

"Oh, come on. Bud's not so bad, and Bryan's a little cutie."

Amy rolled her eyes. "You don't live with them. Bud drives me crazy, always getting into my stuff. He does it on purpose just to bug me. We fight all the time."

"Holli does the same thing. She gets away with a lot because she's little." Heather punched the pillow viciously in the "throat," then sat back on her feet. "I guess that's as good as it's going to get. It doesn't have a mouth or nose, so you'll just have to pretend."

"Okay. What do I do?"

"First you check to make sure the person's not breathing, and that nothing is stuck in their throat. If not, you tilt the head back"—she bent the top of the pillow backward to demonstrate—"and pinch the nose shut."

Searching for the pillow's nose stopped her for a moment. She finally settled for a pinch of pillowcase.

"Once you have the nose pinched shut to keep air from leaking out," she continued, "you blow into the mouth, like this."

As Amy watched intently, Heather bent over the pillow and puffed a big breath into its invisible mouth. Her face was flushed as she lifted her head and added, "You have to do it two or three times, really quick." She gave the pillow two more life-saving breaths for good measure, then sat up.

"Can I try?" Amy asked. "You just watch and make sure I'm doing it right."

Heather nodded, and Amy reached for the pillow. Tilt head, pinch nose, breathe into mouth, she told herself. It sounded easy enough. Under Heather's watchful eye, she went through the steps.

"Great!" Heather said. "Next you unpinch the nose and and listen to hear if they're breathing."

Amy giggled. "If this pillow is breathing we're in big trouble." But following Heather's instructions, she put her ear to the pillow's mouth and pretended to listen.

"Nope," she reported after a moment. "Not breathing. What now?"

"Now you push down on the chest to make the heart pump." Heather looked at the pillow doubtfully. "You're supposed to push on the person's breastbone, but we'll just have to pretend. Your pillow doesn't have bones."

"Thank goodness for that," Amy muttered.

Heather scooted the pillow closer. "Okay, here we go. First you put both hands, one on top of the other, on the breastbone. That's the bone kind of in the middle of your chest—the one all your ribs attach to," she explained.

"Got it," Amy said.

"All right. So let's say the pillow's breastbone is about *here*." She picked a likely spot on the pillow's chest. "What you do is, you press down pretty hard so it kind of mashes the heart. Like this." She pushed down sharply on the pillow, then let go. "You do that fifteen times in a row."

"Why fifteen?" Amy asked curiously.

"I don't know. That's just what they taught us in school. Anyway, you do that fifteen times, then pinch the nose and do the two-breath thing again. That's it. You just keep repeating the two breaths and fifteen chest pumps."

Amy was practicing the chest pumps on the pillow. "I don't think this pillow is going to make it," she observed. "How long are you supposed to keep it up?"

"Until they start breathing by themselves, or until an ambulance or something comes. You're not supposed to give up on them."

Amy knocked the pillow aside. "Well, I'm giving up on this pillow. It's dead, and my arms are tired."

They both laughed. Amy stretched, then leaned back and hugged her knees. "You know what?" she asked dreamily. "Wouldn't it be weird if I had to use this sometime soon?"

"Yeah," Heather agreed. "That would be weird, all right."

"Amy? Me and Bud and Holli are going to play on the rope swing, okay?"

"Uh-huh," Amy said. It was the next day, and she was back at home baby-sitting her little brothers. Heather had come over to play Super NES. They were both concentrating on killing each other.

Amy didn't look up when Bryan ran back into the house a few minutes later. "Amy!" he said excitedly. "Bud is hanging in the tree!"

Amy flapped a wrist at him. "That's nice, Bryan. Now go back outside and play."

She heard the clink of silverware in the kitchen. She thought vaguely that Bryan must be fixing himself a snack. A moment later, the sliding glass door leading to the backyard thumped closed. The house grew quiet again except for the Super NES.

"Ha! Gotcha!" she gloated as she made Heather's man explode in a fireball. "I'm ahead now!"

The sliding glass door thumped open. This time Bryan and Holli burst in together. Bryan ran over to Amy, his eyes wide.

"Amy, Amy, Bud's all blue!" he exclaimed. Beside him, Holli was jumping up and down with anxiety. "Hurry!" she pleaded.

Amy's heart lurched. Bud was *blue?* She dropped the game controller and leaped to her feet. Heather also jumped up. Bryan was already running for the glass door. They followed him, too scared to talk, even.

Two wooden steps led down from the back porch to the grass. Amy flew down them, then followed Bryan as he turned to the right. The tree with the rope swing was just ahead.

Amy screamed when she saw Bud. He was on his knees at the foot of the tree, his back to them. His head was lolled sideways, his knees just brushing the ground. The rope swing, tied to a branch about ten feet overhead, led straight down to his neck. His arms were dangling limply by his sides.

"Bud!" she shrieked. *"Bud!"*

With Heather, Bryan, and Holli at her heels, she sprinted over to her brother. As she got closer, she could see that his ears and neck were a dark, ugly purple. She felt like she was going to faint.

"Heather! Go call 9-1-1!" she screamed. "Hurry!" Heather wheeled around and started back toward the house.

Holli was crying. "Bryan got a knife from the kitchen and tried to cut the rope, but it was too hard," she sobbed. "We couldn't do anything."

Amy was sick with panic. Reaching the tree, she knelt beside Bud. His face was too awful to look at. She forced herself to concentrate on the rope instead. She couldn't get hysterical. She had to help Bud.

The rope was tangled twice around his neck, digging into his throat. She had to get it off! Scooping her brother up with one arm, she used her other hand to claw at the rope. Bud weighed almost as much as she did, so it was hard to hold him up. It took several clumsy attempts before she managed to unravel the rope from around Bud's neck.

"Get back!" she shouted to Bryan and Holli. Bud was a deadweight in her arms. She laid him down on the grass. One look at his blue face and unmoving chest was enough to tell her that he wasn't breathing. She began to sob.

"Bud!" she screamed. "Bud! Wake up!" Almost without thinking, she tilted his head back and pinched his nose closed the way Heather had taught her. She took a deep breath, covered Bud's mouth with hers, and forced her breath into his still lungs. She lifted her head long enough to suck in another breath, then puffed into Bud's mouth again. His chest rose slightly, but he still wasn't breathing.

"Bud! Come on, *breathe*!" Amy let go of his nose and put her hands on top of each other in the middle of his chest. She pressed down hard and fast, counting aloud: "One! Two! Three . . ." all the way up to fifteen. Then she pinched Bud's nose again and puffed into his mouth two times.

Nothing happened. He still wasn't breathing. Amy stared down at him, her eyes blurred with tears. It wasn't working!

Then she remembered Heather's words: "You're not supposed to give up on them." Amy put her hands on Bud's chest again and started pressing. "One! Two! Three . . ."

Across the street, Heather Davis listened impatiently as her mother told the 9-1-1 dispatcher that a boy had been accidentally hanged. Finally, Mrs. Davis hung up the phone.

"They said an ambulance is on the way," she said. "Let's go see what we can do to help."

Heather was in tears. "Bud looks dead, Mom."

"Don't say that! You can't give up on people. Just pray for a miracle."

Amy had reached "Ten" in her chest presses when she felt Bud's chest move beneath her hands. She drew her hands back.

"Bud!" she yelled. "Bud, are you all right? Can you hear me?" Bud made a strange growling noise, but didn't open his eyes. Amy put her hand in front of his mouth, and felt his warm breath brush her palm. He was breathing!

"You're gonna be all right, Bud," Amy said tearfully. "Everything's gonna be okay."

Just then, Heather and her mom ran around the corner of the house. "The ambulance is coming!" Heather called out.

Amy nodded. "I got him breathing, but he's making funny noises. It sounds like there's something wrong with his throat." She looked down at Bud. The blue color was starting to go away a little. Or was it? It was hard to tell.

"Do you want us to stay here with Bud while you go inside and call your mom and dad?" Mrs. Davis asked.

"My mom's probably on her way home already, but I can call my dad."

Debi Toole was glad to be on her way home. It had been a long day at work. She was looking forward to seeing the kids and relaxing for a while before dinner.

She saw and heard the Fire Rescue Unit at the same time. It screamed down the road past her, sirens wailing. In that moment, an icy hand gripped her heart.

*Something's happened to the kids.*

She didn't stop to question how she knew that with such certainty. She just jammed the gas pedal to the floor and took off after it.

• • •

Amy was starting toward the house to call her dad when she heard sirens turning onto their street. She turned around. The ambulance workers might need information about Bud. For now, taking care of him was more important.

A moment later, an ambulance screeched to a stop in front of the house. Amy ran around to wave them into the backyard. They slid a stretcher out of the ambulance and followed her.

Bud was still making growling noises, and now his head and legs were twitching. As the ambulance workers moved Bud onto the stretcher, Amy was shocked at how blue he still was. Had she just been imagining that his color was getting better? Should she have kept breathing into him?

"We need a Trauma Hawk," one of the men said. They began to strap Bud onto the stretcher to keep him from jerking around. "He needs to be airlifted to St. Mary's. Radio for the Hawk to land at the end of the street, away from the power lines."

Bryan was standing next to Amy, pressed against her side. She put her arm around him. She was trembling almost as much as he was.

"I'm going to call Dad, Bryan. I'll be right back." Amy ran inside and punched in her dad's work number. When he answered she blurted out, "Dad? Bud's had an accident. You need to go to St. Mary's Hospital."

Mr. Toole sounded stunned. "I'm on my way." Amy

was glad he didn't ask a lot of questions. She was afraid she'd start crying.

She ran out front to wait by the ambulance. They were bringing Bud around on the stretcher. She looked up when the Fire Rescue Unit turned onto the street. Her mom's car was right behind it.

"Oh, no," she muttered to herself. "Mom will freak out if she sees Bud."

Amy ran over as her mother sprang out of her car. Mrs. Toole was crying and scared. Amy whirled her around, trying to block her vision of Bud.

"Who's hurt?" Mrs. Toole asked in a panic. "What's happened?"

"Bud had an accident, Mom, but he's going to be okay. Everything's going to be okay."

"I want to see him! Where is he?" Mrs. Toole was hysterical. Amy kept a firm grip on her.

"Don't, Mom. Just stay here and calm down."

A police officer walked over just then. "Mrs. Toole?"

"Yes!" she almost screamed. "Will you please tell me what happened? Is my son all right?"

"Well, ma'am, it looks like he was swinging on a rope and got himself knocked out . . . maybe slammed into the tree. The other kids that were playing with him say he'd been jumping off a plastic recycling bin earlier. He might've hit the tree and started spinning. Anyway, the rope ended up tangled around his neck."

"Around his *neck*? Oh, no. . . ." Mrs. Toole moaned. Amy took a firmer grip on her. She was swaying, looking like she was ready to faint.

"He's breathing," the officer said quickly. He nodded toward Amy. "Apparently thanks to your daughter here. Your neighbors say she performed CPR and revived him."

Mrs. Toole looked at Amy in confusion. "CPR? She doesn't know how to do that."

A strange look crossed Amy's face. "I learned it last night from Heather."

Bud was on his way to St. Mary's Hospital in a Trauma Hawk helicopter. Since Mrs. Toole couldn't go with Bud in the Trauma Hawk, another neighbor had offered to drive her to the hospital. Amy had stayed behind to watch Bryan and to wait for her father's call. By now he was on his way to the hospital, too.

Now, with all the ambulances, police cars, and people gone, Amy suddenly felt shaky. She was glad Heather and Mrs. Davis had stayed behind with her.

"Can we go to your house for a while?" Amy asked. "I don't like being here right now."

"Sure," Mrs. Davis said. "Come on, Bryan. You can play with Holli at our house, okay?"

Bryan had been amazingly quiet. "Okay," he said. Together, they all walked slowly across the street. Amy kept an arm around Bryan. Bud's accident had made her realize how quickly things could happen.

"Amy?" Bryan said. He sounded troubled. "I tried to help Bud. I got a knife and tried to cut the rope, but I couldn't. Then I tried a fork, but that didn't work either."

Amy stopped and picked him up. "You did your best, Bryan," she said, hugging him. "I should've listened to you when you tried to get me the first time. It wasn't your fault."

The little boy leaned back in her arms so he could look at her face. "I should've had a bow and arrow. Maybe I could've shot him down."

Amy smiled. "I don't think that would have worked, Bryan. You might have shot Bud instead of the rope."

"Oh, yeah."

Mrs. Davis reached over to pat Bryan's back. "He'll be okay, honey. Don't you guys watch *Rescue 9-1-1*? They always make it."

Amy and Bryan watched TV at Heather's house for a couple of hours, then they decided to go to another friend's house down the street. Heather went along. They were all watching TV there when the news came on. To Amy's surprise, they started talking all about Bud—only they called him by his real name, "Richard." Bud was just a nickname.

Amy listened intently as the reporter explained how "Richard" had been playing on a rope swing when it somehow became tangled around his neck.

"According to the police," the reporter said, "it was

Richard's older sister who revived him by using CPR. The ten-year-old is reported to be in a coma, and remains in critical condition at St. Mary's Hospital."

*A coma. Critical condition.* The words made Amy's stomach knot. Weren't those the things they usually said when somebody was dying?

"Amy?" It was her friend's mother. "You've got a phone call."

"Is it my mom?"

"No . . . it's somebody named Dan."

Dan was a good friend of her father's. Amy took the phone and said, "Hello?" She listened for a minute, then nodded her head slowly. "Okay. Yeah, I guess so. I'll—no, I changed my mind. I don't think I want to go right now. But thanks."

Heather looked up when Amy walked back in. "What did he want?"

"He was on his way to the hospital, and my mom and dad asked him to see if I wanted to go. He was going to come by and pick me up."

"You don't want to go to the hospital?"

Amy looked miserable. "Part of me wants to, but the other part doesn't. *You* saw the way Bud looked. I don't want to see him like that again. Ever." Her hands were trembling. She clasped them to make them stop.

Heather shrugged. "Yeah . . . well, it's not like you can do anything else for him right now. You'd probably just be in the way if you went."

Heather always knew just what to say. Amy nodded gratefully. She sat back down in front of the TV, not really seeing it. Her mind was filled with a silent plea: *Please let my brother live* . . .

Amy and Bryan spent the night at a friend's house, but Amy couldn't sleep. Every time she started to doze off, she'd see Bud's blue face again. She stared up at the ceiling, going over and over what had happened.

*Why didn't I watch them all more carefully?* she asked herself. *If I'd been baby-sitting for somebody else, I wouldn't have been inside playing a video game while they were outside. If Bud dies, it'll be all my fault.*

She rolled over and buried her head in the pillow, trying to block out her own thoughts. She was still like that when the sun came up on Saturday morning.

"Amy? It's Mom."

Amy sleepily held the phone to her ear. Her head was pounding, and her eyes felt swollen. At first she couldn't remember why she was in a strange bed. Then it all came back like a sharp kick in the stomach: *Bud.*

"How's Bud doing?" she asked anxiously.

"About the same. I just wanted to check on you and Bryan to make sure you're okay."

Amy wasn't sure if she felt relieved or upset at the news. "We're all right. Are you and Dad doing okay?"

"About as good as you'd expect, I guess. Listen, if you want to come up here to the hospital, we can get somebody to bring you."

"No! I mean, not yet. Maybe later."

"Okay. I'll call you later, then. Love you."

"Love you too." Amy hung up the phone, then went into the bathroom to wash her face. Her reflection in the mirror looked like a stranger. Yesterday at this time her biggest worry had been what to wear on the first day of school. Today she felt like she was a hundred years old.

She went through the day like a machine, feeling numb inside. Her parents called a few times to check on her, but each time the news about Bud was the same. He was still in a coma. The doctors didn't know if he would come out of it.

Thinking about Bud made Amy's stomach hurt. She had never really thought much about him as *him*. He'd always just been there, like the couch or the stove, a skinny ten-year-old with freckles. Now, thinking of him as Richard Charles Toole, she suddenly realized what good "friend material" he was: a good listener, polite, always ready to help anyone who needed it. The trouble was, she had stayed so busy fighting with him over little stuff that she'd missed all that.

Tears welled in her eyes. If she got another chance,

she'd make sure they were friends. *Let Bud be okay*, she prayed again. *Please don't take him away.*

She waited by the phone all afternoon, willing it to ring with good news about Bud. Finally, late that evening, the phone rang again. Amy snatched it up.

"Your brother's coming out of the coma!" Mrs. Toole said excitedly. "His eyes are open, and he's trying to talk!"

Amy felt dizzy with relief. "So he's going to be okay?"

"The doctors won't say anything for sure, but they're all really happy. I don't think they expected him to come out of the coma."

Amy took a deep breath to steady her trembling voice. "How—how does Bud look?" she asked.

"Well, he's got tubes sticking into him everywhere, but other than that he looks okay. A lot better than he looked yesterday, that's for sure."

Amy shuddered, not wanting to remember. "Can I come see him now?" she asked.

"Sure! We'll send Billy right over to pick you up." Billy was another family friend. "You'll have to ask somebody to baby-sit Bryan, though. He's too little. They won't let him in the Intensive Care Unit."

"I'll get somebody."

Thirty minutes later, following Billy into St. Mary's Hospital, Amy wondered if she was ready for this yet. Her hands were shaking and she felt sick again.

*I wonder why I wasn't shaking like this yesterday while it was all happening?* she thought, clamping her hands to her sides. *I was scared, but I didn't get hysterical until after they left with Bud.*

"Are you okay?" Billy asked. "You're not usually this quiet."

"Yeah. I'm just nervous about Bud."

The elevator doors opened. Billy stepped out and motioned to the left. "This way. You have to wash your hands and put on a hospital gown before you go into the ICU."

When Billy turned into the ICU waiting room, Amy followed. The first person she saw was her father. He looked up when they walked in. His face was tired, and he had huge black circles under his eyes.

"Dad!" Amy cried. Without warning, she burst into tears. She hurled herself at him, burying her face in his shirt. He put his arms around her.

"Hey, it's okay," he said, stroking her hair. "Bud's doing better now. Didn't your mother tell you?"

Mrs. Toole was in the corner, using the waiting room phone. She waved encouragingly at Amy.

"Y-y-yes," Amy sobbed. "I was j-just so scared!"

Mr. Toole nodded. "Me too. But if you want to go in and see him, you're going to have to stop crying."

Amy swallowed and hiccupped a few times, trying to stop her tears. It took a few minutes, but she finally got herself under control.

"Okay, I think I'm ready now," she said.

Her father took her to the scrub room and showed her how to wash her hands. "They keep the ICU as germ-free as possible," he explained. "Now just slip on a hospital gown and you'll be set."

Mr. Toole led Amy into the ICU. "They only let two people in at a time. Your mother will have to wait until one of us comes back out."

She spotted Bud across the room and pasted on a smile. Bud didn't turn his head as they walked up. Amy felt the smile freezing on her face.

*Don't cry*, she told herself. *Just don't.*

She slowly walked to Bud's bedside, noting the snake-like tangle of tubes attached to his arms and body. When she looked at his face, though, she saw that his brown eyes were slanted toward her. A large tube in his mouth kept him from talking, but it looked like he was trying to smile around it. His face was pale white, the ghastly blue color completely gone.

"Hi, Bud," she said weakly. "How are you doing?"

He blinked, then moved one hand out from under the covers. Looking Amy in the eye, he gave her a clear "thumbs-up" sign.

## ONE YEAR LATER . . .

"Over here!" Amy screamed, waving her arms. "I'm clear! *Throw the stupid ball, Bud!*"

Bud dodged Josh and Matthew, then ducked as Heather tried to grab him. When a space opened up, he shot the ball straight at his sister.

Amy caught it neatly, the football slapping her palm with a solid *thunk*. She tucked it under one arm and ran it all the way to the winning touchdown.

As her team broke into a victory dance in the dirt road, Bud ran up to congratulate her. "Way to go! That was a great catch!"

For a long time after the accident, Bud couldn't do much. His injuries left him with bad headaches and some other problems. But he was alive and still working hard to recover.

Amy shook her hair out of her face and grinned back at Bud. "You passed it right to me. I might pick you for my team from now on. You're all right."

"I'm *great*," Bud corrected her with a grin. "Not just all right."

They started toward the house, passing the football back and forth between them. "No, I'd still say 'all right.' "

"Great."

"All right."

"Great."

They were still happily arguing when they went inside and closed the door.

Kids! Have you heard or read about someone who should be a "Real Kid"? We're always looking for new stories for future volumes of *Real Kids, Real Adventures*—true stories about young survivors and heroes. If you've heard about a story that might work, send a newspaper clipping or other information to:

REAL KIDS, REAL ADVENTURES
STORY TIPS
P.O. BOX 461572
GARLAND, TEXAS 75046-1572

You can also E-mail us at: *storytips@realkids.com*. Remember to include your name and phone number in case we need to contact you.

If your story is chosen for use in a future volume of *Real Kids, Real Adventures* (and you were the first one to send that particular story in), you will receive a free, autographed copy of the book and have your name mentioned at the end of the story.

Visit the Real Kids Real Adventures™ Web site at:

http://www.realkids.com

# Win a free

# EUROPEAN ADVENTURE

# or a DYNO VFR BIKE!

If you're a "real kid" who loves adventure, this is the contest for you! To enter, just write a story or essay on the subject: "My Greatest Adventure." Winners will be chosen from two age categories: 8–12, and 13–17.

The winner in the 13–17 age category will join other adventurous teens and professional guides for an exciting 21-day summer European adventure, sponsored by Venture Europe. If you win, you'll go white-water rafting and canyoning in France...mountain biking in Italy...backpacking across vast Alpine glaciers and peaks in Switzerland. It'll be three weeks of nonstop adventure!

The winner in the 8–12 age group will win a brand-new Dyno VFR bicycle, complete with a *Real Kids, Real Adventures* helmet, knee pads, and backpack survival kit. If you win, you'll be prepared for adventure wherever you go!

## CONTEST RULES:

1. Your story or essay must be 1,000 words or less (or a maximum of four, double-spaced typewritten pages). It can be either fiction or nonfiction. Your entry must include your name, age, birthdate, mailing address, phone number, and the name of your parent(s) or legal guardian. Only *one* entry allowed per person.

2. **The deadline for all entries is April 30th, 1998.** Entries postmarked after April 30th will not be considered, and no entries will be returned. Entries should be mailed to: *Real Kids, Real Adventures Contest*, P.O. Box 461572, Garland, Texas 75046-1572.

3. The winner in the 13–17 age category will receive a free "Ultimate Alps" adventure trip from America's Adventure/Venture Europe. Round-trip airfare to Geneva, Switzerland, to meet the Venture Europe team will be provided from the nearest international airport in the U.S. or Canada.

4. Travel costs for transporting the winner to and from an international airport will be the responsibility of the winner's family. Some physical/legal restrictions apply relating to a winner's participation in the Ultimate Alps adventure. All prizes are nontransferrable. All prizes must be redeemed by **August 1999.**

5. The winner in the 8–12 age category will receive a free Dyno VFR bicycle, complete with a *Real Kids, Real Adventures* helmet, knee pads, and backpack survival kit.

6. This contest is open to all U.S. and Canadian residents ages 8–17. Void where prohibited by law. Sponsored by America's Adventure. The Berkley Publishing Group and its affiliates, successors and assigns are not responsible for any claims or injuries of contestants in connection with the contest or prizes.

America's Adventure, Inc.
2245 Stonecrop Way
Golden, CO 80401-8524, USA
Email: adventur76@aol.com
http://www.realkids.com/AA-VE

Venture Europe
Kerkstraat 34, B9830
Sint-Martens Latem, Belgium, Europe
Email: roelver@pophost.eunet.be